Your Tears Are My Problem

They never fell for me

notionpress
.com

Your Tears Are My Problem

They never fell for me

Vikas J.Bhatti

notionpress.com

Notion Press

5 Muthu Kalathy Street, Triplicane,

Chennai - 600 005

First Published by Notion Press 2015

ISBN: 978-93-84878-84-9

Dedicated to
My parents, family, classmates, roommates
And my only love

Based on real life incidents

Acknowledgements

My debut novel *Your tears are my problem, they never fell for me* is all about incidents in my real life. I never thought to write about my boring and dull life until she came in my life. I would like to thank:

- The readers, who helped me by buying this novel.
- My first reader and editor
- Every living character in the book
- Friends who helped me psychologically and economically
- Interesting college faculty and students
- My parents and family, who have always helped me, even in horrible situations
- My brother Jolly, for his *motivational* quotes
- My college mates who gave me the guts to stay at college for four years and always made fun in class and outside. Missing them
- My roommates and close friends, who helped me and filled me with courage
- And my *life* without her where should I find myself. She gave me a reason to live life and face the circumstances

I was happy the day I began writing, completing only two pages in a single day. I wondered at the time that would take to complete the writing.

The book is inspired by my own family and friends. But it should be seem as a work of fiction. The story is based in rural society in North India and features people who are against love marriages. It also focuses on people who think that 'love' is a thing to use and throw.

So, with that I would like to welcome you to *Your tears are my problem, they never fell for me.*

Prologue

'Give me the bottle. You were never a drunk! When did you start this habit?' Arun asked, when I was in a Devdas-like condition. He had returned from Delhi after three years. He was my mamaji's elder son and had completed his CIPET diploma. Now he wanted to give me boring lecture on drink and its harmful effects.

'You were never so interested in my life. So what's new today?' I retorted.

'Vicky! I'm serious.' His eyes were looking worried as well.

'So, for sure you think you have to book an emergency ward,' I said, thrusting my face close to his. He turned his head away – he must have smelt the drink on my breath.

'Your mouth smells like the town's gutter. When did you last brush? Vicky, get up and please come with me.' Arun wanted to give me a job in his uncle's factory. I'm not a laborer; I'm an engineer, a computer engineer at that.

'Who, motherfucker, says that you have to smell my mouth?' I said rudely. I had never done this to him before.

Patchaak! A stinging slap landed on my left cheek. He had slapped me! He is my younger brother. How could he slap me?

'Will you sober up or not?'

'Ouch! What happened to me? Am I all right?' I was reeling from the blow. I put a hand on cheek. This had not happened to me since school.

'You must be fine. You tell how you are feeling,' he said.

He helped me to the bathroom. After my bath, we left for the market. It was evening. Pooran market was crowded. We bought some snacks and then turned towards Bamboo Rest–o–mania. Really, time turns full circle. He once played in my lap and today, he slapped me. One of the worst episodes in my life.

'Chowmin, two full plates, with two black–partridge beer,' I ordered for both. He gazed at me surprised. I asked him the reason.

'What happened Vicky? Tell me…. You never touched these things in your whole fucking life, then why now? Have you noticed your condition? And what are you doing here? Why are you not in the village with bua and fufaji.' He threw these words at me like bombs. I forgot the first one then second and then next. Oh! Why were we here? I rested my forehead on the table.

'Slow down, I don't remember what your first question was,' I said and asked him to repeat.

'Okay, first why are you here in Charkhi Dadri?' Arun asked.

'Because I left my home,' I said.

'Why you drinking?' He shoots another question.

'Because I like it. What happened, you also drink, don't you, yaar?' I cornered him.

'Kanchan? Who is she?' he totally stunned me now. I kept quiet and he asked again, 'Tell me!' The waiter came with two plates and bottles with opened caps.

I think Jolly must have given him the information. He is my brother but he is like an opponent. What was the necessity to tell Arun about her?

'Who told you about her? Please, the next time, don't speak the name in front of me.' I took a sip of the beer and started eating the Chowmin. 'You know, the sweetest girl ever I have seen in my whole life. Let it go. I don't want to talk about her.'

'And what about Smriti and Amandeep Kaur. Who are those girls?' Arun asked another question that left me stunned. 'I have full information.'

'Jolly, I will kill you bro,' I murmured.

'So?'

'So what?'

'Tell me yaar, am I nothing to you?'

'Okay. I met Kanchan and I…' I started and paused.

'From the beginning,' Arun ordered.

1

Okay! The last day of school… that's an awesome flashback. It was my last meeting with all my close friends. I happily gave thanks to all who had given me a chance to top the class. Because they were losers and I was the person, who got 59.80 percent. Were they not? Anyway, they are my friends and now we had to be serious about our careers.

Now I am taking you to my past. The day when I forced my papa to admit me in city school - that's my best wrong move ever. Papa refused. A few of my friends were taking admission there and this was making me want to do the same. In the higher secondary classes, I was the best student and for that reason I thought I deserved something better than the school I was in, but papa refused. I was not a topper but my creative imagination was the best.

I wanted to forget all my previous affairs, my friends, some close friends and some family members. It may sound ridiculous, but I had two girl friends at that time. Those were not only affairs but my life. And at that time, for sure they were my life.

The first one was Navita my classmate. I wanted a meeting with her one last time but I got no opportunity. The last time when I saw her, she was looking more gorgeous than on other days. It was exam time and she was gazing at me. She knew that I was going - she smiled and a tear rolled down. She came to me and handed over a letter. Navita was a simple girl. The first time I saw her, she was sitting on the last bench looking sad, for she was missing her previous school. Likewise, when I saw her for the last time, she was sitting on the floor looking very helpless and of course, worried about missing me.

I went to Bhiwani with a friend named Harmender in search of a school. There were some complexities in this process - no one knew about that school which I wanted to attend. Harmendar was boring with his *pakaau* lecture. He was also forcing me to join his school so he could get assistance in his fee. Nevertheless, nobody, not even the Prime minister of India could make me do that.

'I swear this one is not good,' he said with an evil smile.

'Can you shut your fucking mouth for a few seconds?' I said and this time he was staring at me like he was seeing a monster. He understood that I was not in good mood.

'Ok,' this was his last word.

After a long silence I said, 'Ok sorry… Now would you ask something about that *school*?' This made him happy and made him puff up his chest bigger.

'Hey! Hello! Excuse me,' he called out to a man with a smile on his monkey-type face, 'Do you know where the S.I.T. school is?'

'After the railway station, you will first see the S.I.T. College, then the textile mill, after it will be your S.I.T. school,' the man said. We thanked him and ran towards the railway station.

'Not my school. This is so far, you will fuck up,' he said.

'I love *fuckology*,' I smiled. 'Do you?'

We entered the school via the wide and high steel gate. There was a big *Saraswati* stone statue inside. Two or three rose flowers were near her feet. The peon came forward and asked, 'New admissions?' I nodded. He said, 'Follow me.' We followed him and now we were in a dirty and smelly classroom. Some teachers were sitting on the benches and they were talking to new students' parents. This is a new trend these days - the teacher who filled in more admission forms would get a commission. They were spoiling students' lives by taking two thousand bucks.

'New admissions?' one of the teachers asked. We nodded our heads without speaking. They all laughed and handed me admission forms. I thought they were laughing about their own matters and not at us. *Was I right?*

'I need only one,' I said and I returned the other.

'Only you?' he asked.

I nodded my head again.

Harmender and I came out the room. I completed the form and give it to the same teacher. Harmender was looking for girls outside the door. I tapped his back and he jumped back in shock and whispered in my ear, 'There are neither girls nor beautiful madams.'

'I am not here for both,' I whispered in reply and put an index-finger on lips. He did the same.

He asked the teacher, 'Can we take a look around the campus, sir?' The teacher said yes!

'Come,' he said. We were now in a dark verandah. A few steps down and we saw the sunlight and ran towards it. A very big empty cemented ground was revealed. We drank water while I said that we should return. I tapped

Harmendar's buttocks as I said this and he jumped again. He said, 'Please yaar don't hit me here.'

'Why, is any problem there? Something like *piles!*' I asked. He shook his head.

The teacher gave me a date for joining and we returned home. The school time was 7:45 and because of this, I would have to wake up early in the morning. That was not only difficult for me but seemed impossible thanks to the distance. I was in trouble, big trouble. Bhiwani was thirty-three milestones from my village with tricky roads and the bus was at six. The first day, I reached Bhiwani at 7:35, yet I was one and half kilometers away from the school. Finally I reached and joined the first day second period *fuck me*!

A few of my friends were in section E, the others were with me in F. In my previous school, on students' request, there were only two sections. And here there were sections till F, what the hell!

Section A and B were for arts, C for commerce and D, E and F for science. Ten or eleven science students were enjoying in section E. Section D and F were full with duffers no girl to glimpse. Same situation with commerce only one chick and that was already booked. Only arts and E were lucky.

2

Time slowly went by. I passed the eleventh division with seventy-one percent. My whole time had been wasted in study. I was missing all my *life partners*. When I was doing my ten plus two papa suggested that I stay with a distant bua. He thought that students could study in the home of a family member. But I was not like the others. A dog's tail can never be straightened.

The new session started - we were the *super seniors* now. Early in the morning, I put my books in my bag and reached school. I joined the classes and then went to aunt's (bua's) home. That's when I realised that papa was right. He had always felt that I was a good student.

Little children were playing cricket in the street and for very first time I saw her. In that situation my mouth remained open for a little time. 'Girls…Oh! My! God! They are also here!' I said to myself. I am a dog, really I am. I saw a beautiful face and she was awesome, a gorgeous angel and *patakaa* - you can say. The last word came naturally on my tongue. I had said it aloud.

'What…what was that?' she asked. I kept quiet. My face turned white. That was my first day and I had showed my true colours. Shit!

The next evening, I was struggling with heavy books in my room at bua's house when she came by. 'The Girl Next

Door', I thought of the Hollywood movie. Bua was busy doing nothing watching serials. She came into the house without noticing me, whispered in bua's ear and ran out.

'What's the matter bua?' I asked.

Bua said, 'Nothing.' She didn't want to talk me about it. I understood.

'Okay,' I said, trying to concentrate on a book. But my mind was elsewhere. *Why had she come here? What had she said to bua? Who is she?* These questions were blowing my mind. 'Who is she bua?' I finally asked.

'Oh! Are you okay?' she asked. 'Hmm,' I nodded.

'She is our neighbor from Bihar.'

'But, she is not looking like someone from Bihar,' I asked inadvertently.

'Why? What do you mean by not looking like?'

'She is fair and in Bihar, the people are…' I said.

She laughed aloud and replied, 'She is not of your type, don't think of her.' She laughed again. I did not understand why she told me that.

'I wasn't thinking about her and what's the problem with her? How is she not of my type?'

'Because you are a Haryanvi and she is uneducated too. Your dad will kill both of us.'

'I don't like her. What did she whisper in your ear? That was about me. Was it not?'

'What did you say her today?' she asked. Now I understood. However, I was no really curious about her. *'Was she really from Bihar? What had she really wanted?'*

I shook my head in a '*no*' and I closed eyes to imagine her smiling face. I threw the books aside, gathered the books from the chair and put them in my bag. I sat down on the cot, with my elbows on my knees and my chin on my palms. Blinking my eyes, I saw her. She was the ultimate beauty. I stood up, crossed to the gate. That night I dreamed of her and we were kissing each other.

I forgot Navita totally.

The next morning, I had a big map on my underwear and Capri. What had I done last night? A dirty mind did dirty deeds. Yes, I like her I thought. After school, I stood beside the door. I heard her voice and come out to the door. I looked at her and looked down. She was looking beautiful that evening. When I picked up my forehead, she was staring me. I smirked.

'Shall I go?' she asked.

I nodded with a sweet smile.

'I want to come in, move aside.'

'Oh! Sorry!' I was looking at her big buttocks. They were very big and gently made an arc when she moved. I was speechless when I thought about them. She handed a sari to bua and turned to go.

I called out to her. 'Excuse me! What's your name?'

'Smriti, and you?'

'Vicky, it's Vikram. You are so beautiful.'

She smiled and her right thumb nail was in her mouth. 'Thanks,' she said.

'Ohhhhhhh…' I took a long breath and put my both hands on my closed eyes. Her voice was playing loudly, making my whole body vibrate. '*Smriti*. What a beautiful name!' I kept repeating this. That night I could not get sleep. The next day, I bunked school. That was first time that I missed school for no reason. I was telling myself, 'Cool son! Today she will be yours.' I had no idea how to tell her that I liked her. However, '*Dil Hai Ke Maanta Nahi.*'

After a morning walk I was at the gate when I saw her with a pot full with curd. She smiled and raised it to me. I held the pot and smiled a thanks. She turned and I said, 'Listen! You have any boy…..' and stopped.

'What the hell are you talking about? Am I married? How can I have a boy?' She said, looking at me as if I was the most foolish person in the world. I was speechless again. She turned again and said, '*GADHAA.*' I was staring her ass.

'Sorry! Actually, I was asking if you had a boyfriend. Sorry!' I moved quickly to stand before her.

She stepped closer and said, 'Have you a girlfriend?'

I said, 'No.' I lied because I knew that if I said yes, she would have gone.

'Then, I haven't one too.' she said, shrugging her shoulders and eyebrows tilting up.

'What do you mean by *therefore*?'

'You lied, *therefore* I said,' she emphasized the *word.*

'I lied! I really not have any affairs, okay?' I replied.

'Yeah! You haven't. You always tell this to every girl. Is it not?'

'No.'

'Yes.'

'No, I swear.' Now her eyes went down. I swore and she believed me. How fake could I be?

'Ok! What do you want then?'

'Nothing, just wanna be friends with you. Will you be my friend?'

'I don't know. I really don't know anything about you.'

'I am a good guy and will never make you unhappy.'

'This is what you are telling me. Everyone says this,' she said and walked off, 'I'll think about it.'

'Give me your reply soon,' I said and gazed at her round, shapely buttocks. I saw a real beauty from the back after a long time. Navita was a simple beauty and I loved her. Nevertheless, this one was the ultimate in looks. I knew that if a girl took time to think, it meant that her reply was *yes*. I saw that in many Indian romantic movies. However, there was a fear that if she informed bua, then what would I do. *I will die without her, what will I have left?* That evening, I decided to plead with her to accept of my love. *Love at first sight. Fuck the quotes.*

The watch was running too slow for me. In the evening, she was at the door as I hoped she would be. She smiled at me and I smirked at her. Bua was preparing dessert. She came very close to me, surprising me. She put her hand in her bra and took out a mobile phone. She gave it to me and said, 'Something is wrong with my phone, can you check it out please?'

'You came here only for this *chutiya* mobile!' I abused her. It was unbelievable I had never talked to a girl like that in my whole life. 'I apologize.' I said immediately.

'Never mind,' she said.

'But I do.'

'Why!'

'I told you something early this morning.'

'What? Oh, sorry. You asked for friendship. Is it not?'

'Yeah! Exactly.'

'Ok, we are friends,' she extended her hand. I shook it and thanked her. 'Now will you check it please?'

'Yes, of course.' I long pressed the power button and switched it back on. She thanked me. When she turned, as usual, my eyes went to her buttocks. I called her back, and as soon as she came close, my hands caught her face. I placed a very tight kiss on her lips. That was my first smooch. Forty-five seconds later, I released her. She coughed and hit her fist on my chest.

'What is this?'

'This is my expression of love. I love you a lot and my expectations from you are high too.'

She wiped her lips and went away without looking at me once. I realized that she had rejected my love. I felt guilty and I wanted to apologize. But bua called me for dinner. I stayed leaning on the door, my forehead on the wood. *Shame on me.*

The next two days passed. I did not see her at all.

3

The third day evening, bua gave me the same bowl and asked me to return it to Smriti's house. When I went there, the door was open and I saw her, eyes red due to heavy crying. Had she cried because of me? I stood at the main door and she was in the verandah. I could not face her anymore. She walked forward and I handed her the pot.

'I am sorry Smriti. I didn't have to do that, but I really love you.'

'My mom will be back home anytime. You have to go now. If she sees you here she will kill me.'

'I wanna see you once last time, at my home. You will come, nah?'

'Nah, you proved what you are. I don't want to know you anymore. Please go,' she said.

'I'll wait for you,' I said as I turned to go, 'At the time, when we kissed and at the same spot.'

She didn't come that day. The next day I went to school. I was feeling down. Bijender, my friend, asked me the reason but I couldn't explain. What could I say - that *I made a beautiful girl cry*? I remembered her smiling face the first time I saw her.

'I am selfish person, what did you do Vicky?' I murmured to myself. I returned home after school. What did I see? She was smiling, sitting on my cot. I parked the bicycle and went in.

'Here he is,' she said.

'We were talking about you,' bua said.

'What?' I asked and looked at her.

She replied, 'Aunty was sharing some secrets.'

'Are they about me? If yes, I want to know.'

'Yeah! Something about you when you were a child,' she said with a laugh.

'So what?' I asked and bua stood up.

'I am going for a ladies sangeet. I was waiting for you to come home. You take tea and don't go anywhere. Smriti come,' bua said and moved to the main door.

I nodded and took off my clothes. But Smriti was still standing there. 'Aren't you going?'

'Nah! Is there a problem?'

'No. Sorry for all that I had done.'

'You are feeling guilty. That's enough. But don't do it again.'

'You will forgive me?'

'Yeah!' she smiled.

'Do you love me?' I repeated.

She blinked with a cute smile and looked down. I caught her twenty-six inches waist. I kissed her again without her permission. I was in love and she loved me. *What? She loved me? Then why had she cried?*

'If you love me, then why were you crying?' I asked.

'I didn't weep for you.'

'So?'

'Let it go. You tell how much you love me…'

'Answer me,' I angrily said, 'Why were you crying?'

'For coming here,' she said.

'So, what was wrong in coming here?'

'Mom says that I come here for you.'

'I still don't understand what you are saying…'

'I come here only for you and I think my maa knows that.'

'You come here for me and your mom scolded you for it?'

'Yeah, stupid! No gain, no pain.'

'You really love me.'

'I really love you,' she smiled. I hugged her very tight. 'You don't know how much I love you. I cannot explain.'

'Me too.' I kissed her and released her.

I enjoyed every moment of my life during senior secondary school. She loved me more than she loved herself. I remembered this when I asked her to forget me. She slapped me softly and told me to shut up. The last day, when I was packing my stuff she was with me.

She said to bua, 'Aunty my mom's calling you. You go. I will arrange his stuff.' Bua left. She hugged me tight and my shirt got wet by her tears..

4

I loved her. I would never let her go but that was not in my hands. Everyone says that school time is the best time, but I had a different experience. I don't want that time to come in my life again. Impossibly, I tried to forget her. School time was the best only without her. She came and my result gone. I passed the most important class of a students' life with 59.8 percent marks. I was happy with her but unhappy with result. She came to blot my result. Anyway.........

'She is elder than you as well,' suddenly, I heard a familiar voice - *bua*. The last day of my school, Smriti and I were standing in my room hugging each other and we forgot where we were doing it all. 'And what if she'd be of your age? I told you at first itself that you cannot get her.'

We shocked and let go of each other. Smriti was still crying. I looked at her and said, 'Bua we love each other.'

'I know. I knew it at first and I warned you. What you did was wrong. This all was in your hands – you could have stopped it. You are from different castes, so no other questions arise and you know it very well. Your father will kill both of us. He gave me your to me and I failed.'

'No aunty you have not failed,' Smriti said, 'Vicky you have to go now.' Her eyes were red.

'Sorry bua, I made you unhappy.'

'You didn't my son, this society did,' she said and put her hand on my head.

I picked up my bag and stepped out; Smriti quickly hugged me one last time. I looked at bua and she smiled. Smriti said, 'Promise me that you will never come here again.' I did not reply – I just walked faster. I didn't look behind, tears were in my eyes.

After three months, she Smriti got married. Now she is a mother of two children. Bua told me about her marriage and babies. She was not happy with her hubby. She called me once and I didn't take her call.

This is the end of my second love story.

5

The burden of low marks and lack of knowledge was hampering all efforts to further my career. I wanted to be an engineer, but with the percentage of marks that I had got, a seat was impossible. Girls are my weakness and I got nothing out of it. I was wrong on every attachment with a girl. Boy students' lives are infantile; many things are there to distract their attention. Girls are top on the list. I thought that I would never fall for a girl again. But this thought remains no longer in my brain. Another love story was waiting for me.

Rekha, my cousin sister's marriage was just two months after the last incident. Paramjeet was my cousin's best friend and the only girl who was busy in household there. My *heart called out her name.* After a small conversation she was in my trap. The marriage was over and I started my phone calls to Paramjeet. Affection turned into deep love in just two months.

Daddy wanted me to send for coaching, maa don't want to let me go too far. Grandpa and grandma want to see me become an engineer. Brother and sister were tangled in their own problems. I didn't want to lose one precious year in coaching. I was failure and that was the truth. Parents think that education is straightforward but they will never wonder how we manage the entire burden on our small brain. In my childhood, all I wanted to do was play with boys and girls. But parents will always be selfish. They have no ideas.

One day I went to the city and filled the college application for the first counseling. Harmender was with me. Was he responsible for my failure? Yeah! He was responsible for all of my problems. I hadn't realized this before. Okay The college was relatively new and had been established in 2008. That meant that it was only one-year-old. I searched the website and, wow! It was awesome. I decided to join the college on the spot.

'This is the one,' I said.

'This one is your dream?' Harmender said.

'Yes.'

'Try in second counseling, you must get better.'

'Not better bro,. this one is best.' I said.

'As you wish!'

'See you later.'

'Bye.'

We left the cyber café. He was going somewhere else, so I caught the bus and returned home. I went straight to papa and told him what I wanted to do. My papa is a coconut-type fellow - very rigid from outside but very soft inside. He was with me, at least at this time. But there were many issues in the family - one of which was a *monetary problem*. Rekha Di's marriage, home constructions and now my admission… all at one go. Coaching was a good choice but there were little chances of my success. Because I could complete my coaching from Kota or Delhi but my intention remained the same when it came to girls. I fell in love with babes not books.

Grandpa's retirement fund was running our family. However, everyone told me to pay attention to my studies, not to worry about the problems. I was happy and the happiness could be seen on my face.

6

During my admission grandpa was with me. We reached Ambala at 11 AM. The college campus was cool. I had never seen a college in my fucking life. It had only one building fronted with green glass. The other building was work in progress. I guessed that it could be the hostel being built, but I was wrong - it was also part of the main college building. *"Where is the hostel?" I wonder.* 'Haanji?' A fat, bald and small man, nearly fifty years of age, asked if I was 'new admission'.

'Yes,' I replied as grandpa nodded his head too.

'Nice, come with me,' fatty said blissfully, as if I had accepted a proposal to wed his daughter. He took us into a fully air conditioned room. Mr. Verma was sitting there. He was the management's special *sweet-talker*, who was appointed to increase the number of students. His claver and black tongue always attracts students. I was also going to be trapped.

'Good afternoon,' Mr. Aashish Verma said in soft, buttery tones.

'Good afternoon sir,' I said.

Fatty left.

'Why are you standing just sit down ji,' Mr. Verma said, pushing the ringer on the table. A waiter came in. 'First bring them some water, then orange juice and then a soft drink.'

Grandpa refused all these formalities. 'Ok now show me your documents,' Mr. Verma said to me. I handed them to him. 'So your rank is four thousand.... Sorry, four lakh forty-two thousand and something. It is little far above the ground. No?'

'Yeah, a little,' I mumbled and raised my eyes glumly.

'No problem. Why we are here?' Mr. Verma said. The waiter had not returned. My throat dehydrated.

I was intolerably thirsty and it was hard to hear him barking on unnecessary topics. His image of being loud-mouthed had been frozen for me. Finally, I asked, 'Can I get a glass of water?'

'Waiter!' he shouted loudly. The waiter came and he loudly said, 'For what did I send you outside?' The waiter rudely walked out. We all were shocked, especially Mr. Verma. He mumbled, 'Disgusting people. Anyway you should submit your original documents and we'll return you them to you as soon as you start classes.'

'Why should I need them as if I have already joined a college?' I said.

'Okay, now time's to meet Mr. Perfect,' Mr. Verma said and we left his office.

Mr. Perfect sound like Aamir Khan was waiting for us in another office. I excitedly gulped my spit to wet my throat. I was waiting for a glass of water and nobody was there to give me one.

Fatty came out of another office and asked us to enter saying, 'Director sir will be pleased to meet with you *shriman ji.*' Now I understood who Mr. Perfect was!

'We too, ji!' grandpa said.

Fatty showed us into an air conditioned room, beautifully done up with clean sofas, that smelled good! Mr. Director was speaking on his mobile phone in superfast English. I was staring him with wide open eyes. He looked like a cool dude alright. But I was expecting someone bad like Amrish Puri, in super old age.

'Sit down,' Mr. Director spoke.

'Good afternoon sir.' I said as my high school teacher taught us, respect elders and send respect to God.

'What's your name my son?' Mr. Director asked.

'Vikram, sir.'

'You know sir, this boy has a talent to change humanity,' Mr. Director said to grandpa. This time, it was a little too much. I could not adjust myself on a chair. I got it that he was buttering us. But grandpa fell for his charm.

'Yeah, this is our last hope *shriman ji*,' Grandpa said. I looked into grandpa's eyes, they have a trust. But a fear in heart what if *director was laughing on you.*

'From now, he is not yours anymore. He is our property,' Mr. Director flattered grandpa. How could a college director talk like that? Is there a personal benefit? I was flying in my thoughts and Mr. Director spoke loud, 'yes or no?'

'Yes' I said as shook head in a no. I would not wonder if he asked us for dinner tonight. His expressions were not looking strange but familiar. And the sound of Mr. Director is look alike Hollywood movie dialogues. When a commander salutes and says, 'Mr. President Aliens have attacked New York and stepping fast DC'. .

'So, cash?' Mr. Director whispered, looking at grandpa. Oh! So this was what it was about. Grandpa looked at me. Mr. Director continued, 'The annual fees is sixty thousand six hundred and sixty rupees only sir. If you are paying it in installments, we prefer that you give two, one of thirty-five and the other for twenty-five and six-six-zero. We don't collect donations from rural students. You know very well sir, candidates are very eager to be here.'

Grandpa and I stared at him. This was established in 2008, and in only one year, they were expecting donations too! *Fucking jerks*. In addition, his comment on *rural* - what if we did come from a village, are we not human? Or do we have girlfriends? Time remains not same, what if you are director today. You think you are cool. No, you are not cool. I thought all this but said nothing.

'Yes cash,' grandpa handed him the money. My heart was pumping very fast. I hoped he would return the money saying, '*Your grandson is so intelligent that we are giving him free education at our own cost.*'

He added, 'You can pay the rest after you join and attend your first class.'

I'll feed you my semen now you oldy. I thought not have guts to said that. 'We have already paid the rest of the money - twenty thousand, in the bank. The AIEEE rules,' I said. *You lost the chance.*

'Oh! You could have paid here also,' Mr. Director said.

'Of course sir, but I did it already and now I cannot do anything,' I replied looking into his eyes.

'It's ok!' his voice changed. We stood up to go and Mr. Director give me his hand to shake.

Before we left, Grandpa said, 'And one thing sir, leave alone the orange juice and soft drink, my grandson did not get even a glass of water.' Grandpa said in his Army tone. It was enough to shake every single member of the college. 'Come with me sir ji. They all are busy doing something. I will arrange it for you,' Fatty had entered and he escorted us out.

Sunny weather was burning everything outside. I said grandpa to cover up his baldy head with my gamchha. He refused and combed with his finger, the rest of the corner-sided hairs. He made us sit on aluminum chairs and soon, he handed us two glasses filled with *Mirinda.* Grandpa gave me proud smile as if he had won the war with China. Grandpa, an ex-army guy, always talks about his past life - like how they joined the army in at the age of 15, etc. *When he was my age he got married - he does not tell me about it,* I thought.

'I think that guy was perfect,' Grandpa said, lighting a Covander cigarette without filter. I looked at him, waving my hand to ward off the smoke.

I coughed and argued, 'What perfection?'

'Didn't you feel the knowledge, intelligence, his view towards you?'

'Whatever!'

'Perfect college with perfect faculty,' grandpa said and took a long puff.

This is the way they caught a mouse! You were a fool! I didn't say it aloud though.

'You okay?'

'Yeah! Sleepy!' I screamed.

'So, sleep. Why are you shouting at me?' Grandpa asked, taking another draw of the cigarette.

College was thirty kilometers milestone from the Ambala Cantt. It was 3:45 in the evening when we reached there. We straight visited the railway station. In India, train tickets and food in Parliament are cheap. Unfortunately, we had lost the first opportunity because of bad timing and the second one was not available for us because robbers and corrupts can visit there. We returned and chose the highway for our journey.

'Holly shit! I forgot to take my pen,' I said. 'What? What happened, an accident? Grandpa woke up suddenly. 'You only make these wishes grandpa,' I said.

7

I am a fool. I went to meet Smriti after a long time. I saw her last before leaving for graduation. I found her playing on her lawn with her two-month-old kid. I removed my sunglasses and stood there. I noticed a Mangalsutra around her neck and a sindoor in her hair-parting. I was a bit envious. She picked up the kid and looked at me. I lifted my arms to take him in mine. She wrapped her arms around him as if I was a dinosaur going to eat him. Her face was as bright as before. 'Are you okay?' I asked.

'Why are you here? I told you not to come.' She did not look at me.

'Excuse me! I'm here to visit my aunty,' I lied.

'We both know why you here, no?' she blinked.

'Only to say bye. I'm leaving,' I said. I had no more love in my heart for her. But after seeing her I again wanted to fall for her. The bad part of my heart looking for another chance with her.

'No matter,... you are already gone as far as I am concerned,' she replied.

'You are unhappy to see me here.'

A tear rolled down her cheek and she wiped it as soon I said the words. 'Your presence hurts me even now,' she shrieked.

'How do you think I feel?'

"You are smart and you will soon find your life partner."

"I am not in a hurry," I said.

'You think it was all in my hands.' Her smiley face again turned fishy. 'I had no clued left as you had, Got it. And now you are trying to claim me that I dumped you.' She said.

'Not at all. My sign was not to make you feel bad. I just want to make….. something…. like…… with….. you.' I cleared with unclear words but she understood.

She laughed, 'No chance. Vicky Dickey.'

'What's wrong in it? Even we love each other.' I followed.

'No honey, I love you but you don't. You love pussies.' She used vulgar.

'I had never thought to use you alright. I'll always loved you,' I lied and left. After the marriage she tried to contact me many times but I became selfish and that's the reason behind her rudeness. 'Namastay bua,' I touched her feet in greetings.

'Vicky!' Bua blessed me by putting her hand on my head. 'When did you come?' She was happy to see me I hadn't visited her after the twelfth. She loved me as much as did her own children.

'Good to see you bua.'

'Same here. How is the family?'

'Ah! All are fine. How about yours?' I asked.

'They are all good,' bua laughed. I sighed and bua said again, 'You came here to see me, yes?'

'Any doubt?'

'No. But since Smriti is also here, I asked,' bua teased me with a smile.

'What! Smriti is here?' I pretended to be surprised.

'So, you don't know?' bua made a face.

I wanted to see her face, wanted to kiss her again and obviously, wanted to fuck her. Paramjeet was too far so I thought why not Smriti? But she was not happy to see me this time. I wanted to sleep with her. My elder bro Jolly always says that women are great in bed compared to girls. They have experience. Therefore, I thought, let me try. But I figured out that she was not in the mood at all.

At four in the evening, I wanted to leave. Bua refused to allow me to do so. I wanted to stay on, especially to meet *her*.

'Aunty are you there?' a sweet voice could be heard.

'So she does know you are here.' Bua teased me. 'Yes, I'm here, along with your honey.'

'Stop it, bua. We have not been together for some time,'

'What? No one can forget their first love,' bua said, as I stared at her shocked. *If she is right, then Smriti loves me too.*

'Aunty, do you have any extra *belan?*' she asked. She didn't see me.

'Why? Do you want to hit his head with it?' Bua laughed, so did Smriti.

'Bua!' I exclaimed.

'It's ok. Any problems between the both of you?' Bua asked seriously.

'No matter, you please be quiet,' I protested.

'No aunty, we haven't. I didn't see him at first. That's all.' She explained to aunty.

'Oh! That means that you have meet already. Vicky, you liar!' Bua gave me cunning glance. *Fuck you Smriti.*

'No, actually….a…. bit,' I fumbled.

'You met her a bit, what rubbish! How can you met anyone for a bit?' aunty questioned.

'You came home directly na? Did you not….?' she questioned.

I answered immediately, 'What are you talking about, I don't understand?'

'What were you saying 'you don't know?' Bua asked.

'And you told me that you came to see aunt?' Smriti shot at me.

'Yeah!.... I…. did,' I hiccupped.

'And, what about me?' Bua was angry.

'I came here for both you, please forgive me *deviyo.*' I folded my hands to both.

'It's okay,' bua cooled down. I turned to Smriti. She shrugged her shoulders as if saying *shut your eyes, you loser.*

'I'm sorry too,' she said, blowing my brain. 'Aunty can I talk?'

'When have I refused?' said bua.

She held my hand. I glared. *What the hell was she doing in front of aunt?* We entered the room where I used to sleep during my school days. Bua was far and could not hear us speak. Stuff was where I had left them in the room when I had left. My right arm was in her left hand. She bolted the room door like I was going to escape. Babes don't know about guys, we are ready to bend with them all time. She whispered in my ear, 'Khussssphuussssus.'

'What?' I really didn't hear her. 'Say it clearly.'

'What if aunty is listening?' she said bluntly, kissing my neck.

'She all knows about us. Why these formalities?' I asked.

'I love you,' she replied, offering me her body.

'I love you,' I replied. She was looking unbelievably beautiful and that day, she didn't take a bath also. The mole on her upper lip was covered with dark red lipstick. I wanted to see it before she left and started kissing her. When I let her go, I could see the mole.

'I missed you,' she hugged me. I knew she had really missed me.

'I missed you too baby,' I lied. The best way to impress a girl is to lie as much as you can. Nevertheless, I missed her kisses.

'You know, I always used to ask aunty about you.' She made a face.

'And you got a fucking reply? No?' I quizzed.

After her visit, bua told me that she would be here for one long month. Now I realized *why she changed her mind towards sex with a man who already had left her. She was expecting to screw my dignity. There must be any clash with her in-laws. So her husband was not taking her back home. Trapping plan for tricky buddy.*

I spent that night in aunty's home. Then I travelled back home. The days passed fast and I had to stay away from home for the next four years. Life with family as we are used to it is hard to forget. I am very close to my maa and I would miss her.

8

I had to leave at three in morning, I didn't want to disturb anyone so I left home quietly. It was a cool August morning and the train was at 4:20. I bought a ticket and waited.

August 18, 2009. Morning 6:30.

'Breakfast, where is it?' a hostel-mate came rubbing his sleepy eyes.

'In college.' The warden cum lecturer replied to him while I was busy brushing my teeth.

'Where is college? And why are we asked to wake up so early?' he asked again.

'Do you know who I am?' the warden cum lecturer queried.

'Who?' he rudely asked.

'I am a lecturer.'

'Sorry!!!!!..... sir.' His voice and eyes turned clear.

'Listen! There are twenty-three students in this hostel,' The warden cum lecturer announced. 'So, there is no chance for one round in a mini cab (usually called winger). Students, who are ready will leave first and the rest of them will go in the second round. I'll go in the second as well.'

Only ten were ready including two from my district and school as well. They left in time and obviously they took their meal in time too. I was in the second round.

We reached college cum jail where we were going to waste four precious years at 8:45. We were thirteen along with the warden cum lecturer. We ran toward the mess for breakfast. They gave each of us two *Aloo Paranthas* with tea, a pat of butter. The man serving the butter was digging his nose with his finger, even as he cut the pats of butter with a knife, pushing it onto our plates with his finger. *I had probably vomited.*

I stopped eating butter that day.

'The butter is salty. Ummmm,' said a boy, licking his lips with his tongue. I don't tell him why it is salty. 'You don't like butter?' he asked me.

'I like butter, but not here.' I tore a piece of parantha. It was really messy.

'So, why don't you take a portion for me, mine is tiny. I am starving.' He put his hand on stomach.

I put a pat of butter on his plate. No one was there from my class. I reached the notice board where all the students were looking for their lecture times as well subjects. I followed them and found:

CSE/IT Room No. 302 -Tuesday

8:50	9:40	10:30	11:20	12:10	1:00	1:50- 4:20
Math	FCP	PHY	CHE	M P	LUNCH	CHE LAB
P.R.	S.R.	A.S.	M.K	B.R.	-------	M.K

I checked the time - it was 8:58. I was late and class was on the top floor – I had to take the stairs. *Fuck.* But finally

I reached and what do I see - the class was full. There were almost seventy or more students inside.

'May I come in sir?' I requested.

'Where were you till now? And wear the button - is this a fashion hub?' he asked angrily.

'I'm sorry sir,' I buttoned up my shirt.

'Huuh!!!' he said. I did not understand what he wanted to say.

'Can I come in, sir?'

'I said yes.' He laughed.

Everyone laughed at me, at my dress. I wore a gray bellbottom pant and a shirt of the same color. I sat left to a charming boy and right to a fat and nasty one. I said hello to them and tried to concentrate on what the lecturer was saying.

The day I enjoyed or I enjoyed by the day, were same for me. We spent four months together in hostel.

When the exams were nearly upon us, they threw us out of the hostel. The winter and the exams both were nearly upon us. Fifty percent hostellers had left at a time. Probably, college staff wanted more money to keep us. And during exam time it was a plus point for them by torturing us. I left with my besties Hritik, Jeet and Sid Gujjar. It was a new experience for all of us. We had never cooked or washed clothes ourselves before.

The good thing was that we were all from same state and could properly understand each other. All had a good sense of humor.

Exams were over and we moved to our homes. Six months later I saw my mom. She has a big heart full with emotions. I hugged her she kissed my face and started weeping. Mom! A word that is impossible to define in a single word. Since last two months I and my roommates were preparing our food ourselves and it was appearing on our bodies. And of course mom caught me in a sec. and during holidays she gave me heavy food to eat. She thought that I will have no need to eat for next six months.

The second semester started, one month of holidays passed in a blink. It was second day after we rejoined college. Now our strength reached seven as three Bihari boys came with us.

I got a call on my Chinese cell phone. 'Hello.'

'Hello, Vicky?' a girl's voice.

'Yeah, who're you?' I asked. I was hoping it was Smriti.

'Guess?' she said. It was a trap alright. I was confused now. This is the disadvantage of falling in love with many girls.

'I don't know, and how should I know?' I asked instead.

'Come on, guess!' She said again. 'Achha kinni kudiya nu jaande o.' She spoke in Punjabi..

'Paramjeet!' I got it now. Fatehabad and Sirsa are two districts where Punjabi is an additional language like Sanskrit.

9

'How are you doing?' I asked. We were not in touch since I joined the college. Six months passed and that day she called me. I was missing a girl-partner of course.

'Good. And you?' she asked. She usually never spoke much on the phone. I realized that she was with someone else as she was giggling. I asked her that, but she did not respond properly.

'Tell me, whom are you with?' I asked again, now a little angry.

'Why are you shouting at me?' she cooled down and whispered.

'And why are you whispering?' I shoot another question.

'I'll call you later,' she said and she hung up.

'Liste..n,' I totally said and stopped. *I will call you later as she always does.* I muttered. I tried Paramjeet again but she didn't take my call. I wondered why. Was she with someone? I tried again for the next ten minutes. I got the message by a sweet sounding lady - *the number you have dialed is currently switched off, please try after some time.* I let it go.

That evening, I was at a party and the phone rang again.

'Hello. Why did you hang up?' I asked her.

'Cool baby, you become nervous fast. That was because I had relatives visiting here,' she lovingly replied.

'Who?' I asked.

'My mama ji and his friends,' she answered.

'For what?' I asked.

'To see me,' she said simply, playing down the fact that it had been a bride-seeing ceremony.

'And what did they decide?' I asked in a sad voice. She was eldest of her siblings. Marriages in her community are like if girl marriages a boy, that boy have to fix marriage of his own sister to his wife's brother. And he becomes sala of his own sala.

'I don't know,' she replied.

'What do you mean by don't know?' I asked.

'I really don't know, mama ji will tell us later.'

'And you are sounding happy. So, that's why you called me today after six months to tell me that you are gonna marry.' I was jealous. No boyfriend in this world wants to see his girlfriend with someone else.

'No,' she said and I hung up this time.

This time, I didn't pick up her calls. I switched off my phone for the whole night.

In two days I got ninety-eight calls from her. The third day was almost gone when I got a call from Rekha Di. I hesitated because I know she had complained for me. I attend, 'Hello.'

'Vicky, what the hell is happening to both of you?' she asked.

'Nothing Di,' I replied in a low voice.

'Are you okay?' she asked.

'I'm okay Di,' I murmured.

'What exactly happened, did she say anything wrong?' she asked about Paramjeet. If you have an elder sister then you no need of a better friend. She can take care you like a friend and a mother.

'She is going to do vyah,' I said.

'No, the date has not been fixed. Is that why you are not taking her calls?' she asked.

'All is over. She is getting married, no?' I said.

'You can take her call at least once.'

'Then what? I don't want to be *dhobi ka kutta,*' I said angrily.

'You are not. Anyway take her call once for my sake , only one time please,' she requested and I couldn't refuse her.

'Okay,' I hung up.

We cousins were very close to each other. So I know that Di was very upset with the Paramjeet matter. I was totally broken up as to why this was happening to me. Every girl whom with I fell in love got married. Do I run a marriage bureau? Di was cautioning me with affection, much like bua did in Smriti's case. Suddenly my phone rang again breaking my chain of thought. I took the call but didn't speak.

'Vicky!' she spoke lightly.

'Speak,' I replied rudely.

'Oh!!!!! I am going to die without you, Vicky. Please forgive me,' her crying shook my whole body. I didn't expect her to be so emotional.

'Hey! Stop crying Param, I am sorry,' I apologized.

'Please Vicky don't do this to me, I'll kill myself,' she wept.

'You love me?' I emotionally blackmailed her.

'Yes goddamn, I do - more than you do me,' she said this and I could hear her sniff.

'Can we elope?' I asked.

'What? You are asking us to run away and get married?' she was surprised.

'Yes, tell me, can you do it?' I asked.

'No. Never, of course.' She confused me now.

'So, let me go then,' I blazed.

'No baby, please don't do this. I cannot handle this.' Her sobbing began again.

'I'm sorry,' I said and hung up the phone.

Our last conversation made me feel terrible. What would I say to Di, for I was sure that she would call me. She did.

'Di, please don't piss off me,' I took her call after a full ring and directly said this.

'You said no to her?' she asked.

'Please let me go, and don't call me back,' I said.

'You saying this to me or did you say this to her?' she confusingly asked.

'I told her this.'

'And?' she expected more.

'What and…? Is this not enough or I call her back for more?' I asked.

10

My college friend and my religion-brother Veer from Rohtak was with me in my room. He is a Majnoo-type person, with many girlfriends and had a lot of affairs with ladies. His agenda was to use everyone, but remain single. At that time, I think that he was serious about Poonam. Rohtak reminded me of an incident when our English teacher was asking us to introduce ourselves in class and he started in Haryanvi-English, 'Myself beer from Rohtak, passed from Jaat school Rohtak.' Obviously he was a Jaat.

Hritik Yadav was committed with one of his neighbor, named Ritika Yadav. In relation they were uncle-niece yet not in same family but village. Five letters were same in their names and he proud on it. In his sight it was a perfect combination of five letters that makes relationship strong. I matched my name with Smriti's and Paramjeet's; it was two and three respectively, means that our break up was predetermined.

Sid Gujjar was six feet and three inch tall with a heavy body. The name Khali was coined by me because he reminded my school friend Anil that we used to call him by this name. He was also in a committed relationship with his brother's saali (sister-in-law) Anjani, who had a round-shaped body like *rasgulla*.

Jeet from Rohtak, was with one of best friend's girlfriend's friend named Preeti. She was of light-brown complexion - even he hated dark-skinned people.

Around me, everyone were busy on their phones – I fooled around a little, listening to their conversations and talking nonsense. I picked up my phone to check for any missed calls - there was nothing. *I am single now, who wants to be mine,* I thought. My mind was in stress; I could not call Smriti or Paramjeet anymore.

In the evening, I was deep in sleep when the phone rang. I picked it up. 'Hello,' I rubbed my eyes. It was an unknown caller.

'Vicky, it's me,' a girl's voice said.

'Who?' I asked.

'Rekha. How are you? I called you at home - you were not there.' she asked.

'I'm fine Di. Is the family ok?' I asked and gargled my mouth.

'Your voice is not clear again, how is it going Vicky. Why don't you talk properly to me? Or am I creating problems for you?' she kept talking.

'No Di, not at all. I was bit sick ,' I lied.

'You know, I am your elder sister and well-wisher also. You talk to me properly,' she knew that I was lying. She was more than a sister to me.

'You know Di, what I am serious about,' I said emotionally.

'You are missing her? Why did you fight with her then?' she asked. She was serious now. She had called me for some other reason and I made her nervous. She said, 'I called to tell that she is going to get married.' and hung up the phone.

I called her back immediately. She picked up the call without saying a word. I said, 'Hello Rekha.'

I could hear her sobbing and this time I couldn't control myself - both bro-sis started a loud howl. If we had been together we would have hugged and wept for a long time. She couldn't speak since she was sobbing heavily. I tried to console her but in vain.

'Listen to me Di, please stop crying. I'm okay here. Please.' I tried to make her feel better.

'I love you, and please call her at once. She is still waiting for your call. Why did you fall for her if you couldn't handle it? This is not her fault. Her family had fixed it - you should not give her grief.' She then hung up. I was unhappy and I knew that Di was also. She is a good woman and always tries to make everyone feel good. But I did the reverse. How did I manage this? I wanted to call her again and say, *I love you my sister, I do care about you. You are the only one who can understand me. Please forgive me and I will do as you tell me to.* For her sake, I decided to make the call. Paramjeet picked up in a hurry.

'Param.' I said.

'Vicky! Hey!' she seemed joyful, and happy.

'How's you? I got news. *Congratulations*!' I greeted.

'Thank you very much,' she said.

'Welcome anytime,' I replied.

'No, thanks for the call. And obviously you will not be welcome her anytime,' she amended.

'I called only to wish you. I hope you'll be happy,' I murmured. *We have not five letters same in our names,* I wanted to say.

'I missed you,' she said. We had been apart for two months. In this time period we never called each other. 'Will you attend my marriage? Please don't say no! It will be hard for you, but please.' she asked.

'When?' I asked.

'14th April. You will come, no?' she asked.

'No. Sessionals…..' she interrupted me.

'You have to come, no excuses. Please Vicky, that's my wedding gift from you. It's the first time that I am expecting something from you. I'm sorry that I couldn't be yours. Please!' she requested me sweetly. How could I refuse her? She was my ex-girlfriend, we had not even kissed each other but we were together; we talked, shared everything, phone kisses and phone sex. What'd I say if I met her? *Wish you a happy married life* or *satisfy your hubby… blah blah.*

'Okay, I'll see,' I said.

'No you have to come; I want to see you one last time. Who knows when we will meet again?' she said.

'Ok,' I agreed. I didn't know why I said that. But if she was happy then I am happy as well.

'Ummmmaahhhha.' She gave me a long kiss. In these two months, I really missed it. This was the end-call kiss or good-bye kiss. I was feeling good now, Di was right.

I was suffering, with the countdown to her marriage date approaching. The day was coming near and I decided to call her once more. But the thoughts in my mind kept me back. *What are you going to do Vicky, mom will kill you. Is that right for your family's dignity? For your own selfish reasons, you are spoiling two families and their lives forever. What if she says yes to eloping? Will you run away with her and leave your family, who share all your dreams? What about your grandpa's hopes?* I stepped back, finally.

11

The date came and she was married and gone - far from family, far from friends, far from relatives and far far away from me. I switched off my mobile two days before the wedding day and did not switch it on till it was over. She must have tried to call me. I was upset but there were other things cropping up as well. The cook's three horny daughters. Reenu, Kanchan and Sweety in top to down order. One of them had not good view towards me. I tried to keep myself out of this after Param's marriage. One of them used to come with their mom to cook every day or to help her in work.

There were six of us in three rooms. Hritik and I were in same room. Hritik was slightly close to me and I told him about Paramjeet.

Reenu was committed to Shiv our senior. Kanchan was with Garv, my roommate at hostel and Sweety… I don't know about her. She herself does not know how many boyfriends she has had. She was only fourteen and she had been with fifty plus boys, *shocking*!

When I broke up with Paramjeet, that day I heard about Kanchan and Garv. They broke up as well. Who did the breaking up no one knows. She used to come to our room for three days continuously. We spoke about what to cook and when her mother could come to work.

One day I got a call from the cook - she was going for a marriage with family and could not return till morning. So, we had to prepare our own dinner. All the Biharis were missing. I could make *rotis*. Hritik was an expert in kneading the flour for the rotis. Gujjar is his type fellow, no work to share but always eager to eat. I requested him to cook rice for all but he cut it from the corner.

'Okay, can you please tell the process to cook rice?' I asked.

'Yeah, why not? But only on one condition.' I knew what he would ask for.

'I know… I will cook for all.'

His voice was now the voice of the expert. He began to give me directions. 'Fill cooker with rice and water.'

'Wow! How clear that is. Do one thing, go and sleep tight. I'm not giving you even a grain of seed also,' I said showing eyes.

'I mean, one is to two is the ratio of rice and water.'

I lit the gas stove and placed the pressure cooker on it, following his instructions. I was not used of it so I forgot to remove the cooker. After two whistles I emerged my rice had been burnt. In hurry I got them out and it was eatable since from above only. We thrice ate and rests of us go *to hell.* The rice persons were finding rice in the pot. They were starving as they couldn't live without food for an hour late. When he appeared the rice's condition, he advised me not to cook again.

It was the night shift for the cook. She and Kanchan arrived on time. The cook asked, "Who cooked this rice?" I jumped up in acknowledgment. I expected her to say *very good son, you did a great job in my absence.*

'You burnt it totally *beta,*' she grinned. Kanchan gave me a smirk.

'Aunty, actually I was…..' I stuttered.

'So, that's how people in your town boil rice,' Kanchan laughed aloud.

'I don't have a degree in cooking!' I said in reply, and smirked back at her. She went to wash the dishes and aunty became busy in cutting the vegetables.

'She is grinning. What's the matter?' Gujjar asked.

'Nothing *yaar,* we were just talking,' I replied.

'Are you going or should I go? You know she is single now. I'm saying this because she smiled at you and you are single too,' he asked me.

I was also in his favor. My brother Jolly had already been told me to commitment. I decided to follow her to the hand pump where she was heading to wash the dishes. She useless in pumping the water out. I helped her and the pot overflowed. She said, 'You burnt the rice and now I am going to have difficulty in washing the cooker and the vessel…"

I stopped her tirade with:

'Kanchan, I love you.'

I lied, as village girls expect these words more than the *I like you* or *will you do friendship with me, etc.*

12

'Big Brother knows, no?' she asked referring to Gujjar.

It was ten days since Paramjeet's marriage. I had promised myself that I would not fall in love with anyone in which five name letters not matched. I intended to use her and then leave her. What a bloody dog was I? She was a simple looking Punjabi girl but she was Hindu. She was pretty, but not prettier than Smriti or Paramjeet.

Next fall she didn't come with aunty. I was waiting for her and her ego was touching the sky, I thought. I was not serious for her but a bit conservative. Gujjar and I were chatting around noon when a young boy of age twelve or thirteen called me from outside the room, 'Who is Vicky here?'

I looked at him and said, 'Fuck, I'm gonna flush now.' He was Kanchan's younger brother Shubham. I was sure that aunty had sent him.

'I am!' I exclaimed. I was frightened. He was aunt's fourth-born among her five children. The last one is Vishal. I stood up, went out and asked, 'What happened?'

'Didi wants your mobile number,' Shubham said.

'What the fuck? She sends you to ask for my number? You are her brother, no?' I asked, confused.

'Yes.'

'Kanchan didi wants to speak to you.' That was Sweety's voice. I turned to see her. She had come with him. What type of family is this? I was confused whenever I thought about them. A brother can never ask for the mobile number for his own sister or were they so modern like Americans? In Haryana it was a rare case and that happened with me.

'Oh! Okay. Tell her start coming here regularly,' I said.

'You do it yourself. She will call you when I reach home,' she said. They turned and left. Gujjar and I began chatting again but now topic turned on that family.

I was getting many calls from Smriti and Paramjeet, and now from Kanchan. I had to spend fifty rupees daily to recharge my mobile. A girl is a person whose wallet is never empty. Mamaji, uncle, bua, aunt, grandma, masi and all other relatives hand them money during visits. And they are experts in giving missed calls.

Here, I want to discuss a useless topic, a useless but true fact. Girls love giving missed calls. The size of miss call is one-tenth or one sixteenth the part of a single ring. The sound of the ring even in Chinese phones is, *beep.* No one can hear this sound. Sometimes, I would mistake it for the low battery tone.

13

'Hello' I called her back in reply to her missed call. Kanchan was happy to hear my voice.

'How are you?' she asked me for third time. She had been giving me missed calls periodically. This was her third one and the third time she was asking me the same question.

'I'm sick. My body temperature is at one zero eight,' I replied, tired of saying *I am fine.*

'You were saying that you are okay half an hour before,' she stupidly asked.

'In your absence I have fallen ill,' I said romantically.

'Don't be so *fekoo.* I know you are alright. You are flirting, no?'

If you know then why you asking?, Or do you think I am a fucking jerk? I controlled saying it aloud. 'Yes. You are so smart, clever girl.'

'What did you think – just because I am uneducated, I don't know anything? I'm knowledgeable about you guys.'

Yeah! Of course you do, you had been living in between boys for the last two years. You are an expert, you can to do PhD on this subject. I didn't reply. I couldn't have said all this to her. All I wanted was an affair with her during the span of my college days.

'How many girlfriends have you had?' she asked another silly question. Girls think that boys are fool as foolish as they are. She asked me about my girlfriends, but who is to start counting?

'You are my first and will be my last. What about you?' I queried.

'You know it - it was Garv.' She could not hide it because the whole college knew about it.

'And?' I teased her so that she would tell me more about herself.

'No one else.' She was of course, lying. But I didn't push the point. I knew about her family now. If her brother could play Cupid and ask for my number for his sister, what kind of family would they be?

'Sure!' I exclaimed.

'Yes,' she confidently replied.

'You know, I hate liars. If I get any information from others then I would not like it.' She didn't reply. I said, 'Ok then, chill out.'

Our conversations start growing with time. Two minutes of talk-time now became twenty minutes. My roommates were surprised with my conduct. They all were busy in their lives. I was in mine.

One day, Kanchan called me early in the morning. She said, '..........' I mumbled in my sleep and put the phone down. I have no idea what she said.

When I am sleep I cannot handle anyone or anything. If she was Katrina Kaif, I would ignore her. I checked my pillow - it was between my legs. I use it below my head but don't know when it comes between my legs.

It was seven o'clock when I heard the cook's voice asking about the menu. Hritik was busy doing *Puja.* He never speaks during puja, even if his girlfriend unclothes herself and offers him her body on the condition of one word. . He has four photos - of Lord Ganesh, Lord Shiva and Hanuman Ji and Goddess Saraswati. And behind every photo, there is a purpose. Lord Ganesh was for family peace, Lord Shiva was for control of anger, Lord Hanuman for a muscular body structure and the Goddess, for education.

I got out of bed to instruct her as all the others were still sleeping. Aunty was in the kitchen.

'Where're the girls?' I asked rubbing eyes. I was wondering where Kanchan was. She was absent today. From the day I offered for her, she never bunked a single day. I wanted to check the reason behind her absence.

'Kanchan is working for her aunty now. She will never come here again. Reenu and Sweety are going to another place. I'll manage it all here from now on,' Aunty explained.

I got confused - why hadn't Kanchan told me about it? I tried to gather some more information. 'Aunty who?'

'My neighbor. She has been going there from when she was nine.' This gave me another clue. It meant that she had been a servant from the age when she should have been playing with toys.

The next day, she called me, I didn't take her calls. She kept calling but I did not respond.

After college I took her call, and she shouted at me like she was my wife. I was also in a temper so this shouting made me angry.

'Yes I knew, you would do it to me.' she screamed. When girls are depressed, only this comes into their minds. Sorry boys, that I said 'minds'. They don't have the meaning of this word in their dictionary.

'Oh! it is that so? Wow, hats off to you *Jaan*. You don't come my room anymore, have you any answer why?' I asked.

'I called you at five in morning and told you the reason,' she was extremely angry.

'Okay then what, and what about Garv. You kissed him, no?' I turned the information on her. She was calm now. She hung up the phone. *Beep!*

14

19th May

It was my birth date - Gujjar, Hritik, Nikunj, Nilesh, Ritesh and Veer wished me a long life. I was gonna celebrate it for first time on a big budget. After joining college, this was my first chance to gathered my best friends and throw a party. I invited all my nearest friends including Jelly and Amit from Sonepat. Everyone were enjoying beer while Hritik, Ritesh and I fought for cold drinks and Bhujiya. Gujjar was drinking for the first time. I strictly told him to limit what he drank.

I purchased a carton of sweets for Aunty. Kanchan likes rasgullas and I bought them for her to impress her. I handed it to aunty. She thanked me and promised me a gift.

No need for a gift aunty ji. You had given me your precious daughter. This is enough if she does work properly, I thought. I told her I didn't want a gift – what would my friends think? And who cares what they think, those all tharkee even not gifted me a pencil.

'Beta come home a day for tea.' Aunty said taking the box filled with sweets of one twenty bucks. The tea was not for me but for the box. Otherwise, she had never asked me for tea before.

'Okay aunty I must come one day to annoy you,' I said in filmy style. These type of words grow up your personality.

'What annoy beta, it will be a pleasure.' She said. Her behavior was ultimate. She called beta to every young person and this made her a good lady.

The party-time was over and all the guests had gone. It was time for dinner. Aunty came to cook, a girl in tow. I thought that it would be Reenu or Sweety. When aunty called for me, I saw my beautiful babe there. I thanked aunty for such a beautiful gift, what she promised me in morning.

'Happy B'day Vicky,' Kanchan greeted me. She was looking gorgeous today. I forgot our fight. I wanted to kiss her in front her mother but I controlled myself.

'Thank you, Kanchan,' I replied. She gave me a sweet smile and got busy in gathering the used dishes. She ran towards the hand-pump and I followed her since she winked at me.

'Why didn't you tell me that it is your birthday? I'm sorry for spoiling it with a fight,' she apologized. I caught hold of the handle and pumped it.

I gave her a bitter glare.

'I'm sorry, Vicky. Please forgive me. But I did call you in the morning,' she said.

'Okay, let it go. Where's my gift?' I asked, cutting her. I was expecting a bumper gift.

'What you want?' she shyly asked. She put her hand on mine, 'Stop it now, I need water only for dish-wash, not for a bath.'

'I know you like rasgullas so I bought them for you. Now you get me what I like,' I said. Now she looked confused. She had never asked me what I like.

'No, No. You tell me and I will buy it for you.' She said and easily got out of the trouble.

'Okay, then keep my present pending. When I've need for it, I'll ask you,' I said. She didn't know about me, with the agreement she signed right now I could demand her anything possible for her.

'Anytime,' she laughed and got busy in work.

I didn't see her for one month, we spoke only on calls. Sometimes, she called me and invited me to her boulevard. I saw her, she saw me and we exchanged smiles. We became busy in our lives.

A day she called, 'Hello, can you come to my place?' She seemed in a hurry and hung up the phone. I thought that she must be in trouble.

The day was long, the lecturers fucking us. The next lecture was Manufacturing Process by Bhuvan Ranjan. He is the most irritating lecturer in college, and once he starts no one can handle him. Not even the director. Whenever he entered the class, after the formality of greeting us all, his attention would remain on the blackboard.

After college, I ran and went straight to her home, that had shabby walls covered with dung-mud-paste. A black iron door stood half closed. I entered without knocking since no one appeared to be inside.

'Vicky,' I heard a girl's voice. This couldn't be aunt's, because she did not add *beta*. I turned to see a beautiful face. 'Hi.'

'Where's aunty and others?' I asked.

'Reenu and Sweety have gone shopping and mom has an appointment with a doctor in Barara.' She was smart alright.

I grabbed her behind at her waist. Her waist was only twenty-three inches. She came very close to me. 'Then why did you call me?' I asked.

'I was feeling lonely.' She had brushed her teeth with Pepsodent toothpaste, I guessed.

'And I am cartoon that makes you laugh,' I said and thought; why was I wasting the precious time before nonsense. Anyone could come anytime. I leaned forward and tried to kiss her.

She stopped me saying, 'This is your gift. Never ask for anything more again.' She laughed. She was ultimate in kissing. I didn't let her go until our lips hurt. 'Thanks Vicky.'

'For what?' I asked. Her eyes were red due to kissing. I put my thumb and index finger and squeezed her lips. They were very soft, it was like I was pressing cotton.

'For coming here.' She grabbed me tight and we hugged.

'Thanks for calling me here.'

'I miss you,' she said and kissed my cheek.

'I like you,' she kissed my forehead.

'I cannot forget you,' she kissed my eyes.

'I love you,' she kissed my lips.

'I love you too,' I said and gave her a love bite on the neck. She then chewed my lips and we hugged, promising not to leave each other.

15

I got up early morning when my phone rang. It was Jeet, I picked up the call. 'Hello,' I said in a sleepy voice.

'*Bhai*,' he said. He was sobbing. I woke up then.

'Jeet, what happened?' I asked, as I checked the time on the mobile. It was seven thirteen.

'She kicked me.' He was talking about Preeti. He had been spending a lot of time talking to her and really loved her.

'What? How?' I asked and walked towards the washbasin. In kitchen, aunty was busy kneading flour while I saw Sweety was cutting vegetables. She was looking good in a white dress. When workload increased, aunty brought in a daughter to help her. I could see her eagle eyes on me.

'She is leaving me to go elsewhere for higher education. I tried to call her, but she didn't reply. I cannot live without her. Please tell me what to do.' His voice was breaking.

'What rubbish! What if she going for higher education? Are you a monkey that you will tear her books?' I was upset too.

'Please help me Bhai, I cannot handle the situation alone. I'll destroy myself.' His voice was trembling. He could do anything in that situation, I knew.

'Where are you? Please come here to me.' I ordered him.

'I am in my room,' he said.

'Then come here soon,' I said, 'We will talk in personal.'

But he had started on another topic by then.

'Jai's girlfriend was caught by her mother while they were talking on the phone,' he said. He was really bamboozled. His own predicament and now Jai's had made him really confused.

'What is actually the matter? You are my problem, Jai is not my problem,' I said.

'He is your brother. You have to worry about him,' he said.

'Was. Not now. And please come here soon, we have to talk,' I said. Jai, who had been my best friend till a few months back was not in touch anymore after we left hostel.

'She is not going to come back Bhai.' He started crying again. He was a fucking jerk. First of all, he woke me up so early. Secondly, he reminds me of the person who I don't want to think about. Now he was confused as well.

'Okay then, you'll come here right now.' I hung up. Jeet who never touched wine that day was looking disposition. *Why people fall in love like assholes?* 'She is with someone else, I think,' he said. *I think* wow! What an imagination. He met her last time five months ego. Why was he so mad for her, I didn't know? If she ignores him then fine, kick her and try a new one.

'What?' I asked and looked at Hritik who was still busy in his Puja. Sweety gave me a glance. Aunty had started making rotis. Time was running out and I had to take a bath and get ready for college.

'Give me some idea how to win her back, Bhai. I'll die without her.' He was howling now.

'You are coming to college mad-ass?' I asked. If he annoyed me anymore, I would kill him.

'No, not today. I am going shopping with Saurabh and Garv.' He surprised me now. Was he trying to annoy me?

'Wow! So you are shopping for a break-up gift for Preeti. Bye then,' and I cut the call.

Now I understood why Preeti was leaving him. He made me stressed in twenty minutes then what happened with her in twenty weeks.. He is a good looking and charming young man. But he has no social graces. One day, when we were in the hostel and going to Barara in an autorickshaw to shop, a girl seated just in front of him started teasing him. Like most boys are with girls, he was shy.

As she continued to tease him, finally he lost it when we got down. He started shouting at her. 'You've not got brother-father in your family? What manners did your family teach you? Does your mother do this with everyone? Etc.' He made an ultimate scene in the bazaar. Everyone was staring us. The girl stood like a statue while he barked like a dog. I stopped him and dragged him away from there. If the police came, we would be in trouble, especially since this would be a case involving ladies.

16

Kanchan was calling every minute. She knew that I would be in college. But I was getting aroused – I wanted to screw her.

'Hello darling!' I said romantically after class.

'Whom were you busy with this early morning?' she asked quickly.

'A friend. Why?' I asked. I had bunked college after the third lecture for time with her!

'You were talking with a girl, no?' she asked. I was getting ready for long kisses. I had washed my face with cold water and then chewed a center fresh.

'No!' I never took Smriti or Paramjeet's calls now. Kanchan was sweet and next to me, so why would I waste my money on them? 'No, I don't speak to any girls after I got together with you.'

'Your phone was engaged for half an hour. Am I wrong?' she asked.

'You are right. But I was speaking to my friend who is in a bad situation. Who told you this?' I said.

'Sweety.' The coin dropped. I hate that girl most in the world.

'She is your sister or anything else? Tell me,' I said.

'Give me the proper answer,' she said. She proved that Sweety was more important than me. In her sight every wrong work has been done by boys.

'I had already given you the answer, believe it or not?' I said. After all I'm a man, and cannot behave like assholes. 'I think you are lying,' she said, 'Yes, I believe you but not the girls you have been with before.' She left me astonished. I wondered.

'Girls! I was single and now only with you jaanu.' I tried to sweet talk her. Of course I'm a man, but cannot make her go easily.

'I know everything, no one is single in this world. And you, never. I can bet.' She was making me mad. I was on crossroads, one for Kanchan other for my room.

'Who are with you at home?' I asked standing for her answer and final decision to move on..

'With Sweety. Why?'

'I'm coming there,' I said and disconnected the call. It was a hot afternoon and I could see no one about. It would be a perfect time. The thing I really wanted that moment was to grab her like last time.

I reached her house. 'Aunty,' I called, so that the neighbor would not suspect. Kanchan came out with bare feet. She wore a black salwar-kurta with no dupatta. Her hair was opened and slow combed. Fabric red bangles and black gaani in white neck. Ear and nose ring were same. Her black suit was adding more stars in her beauty.. She looked lovely. I slowly entered the house, looking at her almond-shaped eyes. 'Is aunty here?'

'No, but she will be coming soon.' She dropped her eyes.

'How soon?' I asked in a lusty tone. She looked at me again.

I caught her and planted a kiss on her pink lips. She shut her beautiful eyes. I grabbed her hand and pulled her into her mom's bedroom.

'Mommy will be coming very soon.' she said and exclaimed, 'Why you eating my lips? That hurt!'

'I know.' I was hungry for her. If she was an ingredient, she would be in my stomach already.

As soon as I said that, she bit my lower lip. I cried out in pain and she left it. I checked whether there was blood or not. Thank God! . 'Are you a bitch?' I screamed. 'Yes I'm your bitch my puppy,' she started licking my lips softly. Her expression was fabulous. That's why I was falling for her more and more every day.

'Mommy is coming!' Sweety came into the room and we pulled apart. I sat on the bed while Kanchan took out a water bottle from the refrigerator and handed it to me.

'Namaste aunty,' I greeted her and put the bottle aside.

'Namaste beta, when did you come?' she asked and sat on the chair next to me. Kanchan stood at the door and smiled at me. 'Kanchan, prepare tea for Vicky.'

'No aunty, thanks. I came here to meet you.' I lied.

'He will not even drink water at a poor person's house, mommy,' Kanchan said.

'I do.' I showed her empty bottle and winked.

17

We were busy playing *Antakshri* that evening. Sweety came alone to work. Hritik, Ritesh, Gujjar, Nikunj and Nilesh were at the party. Gujjar asked me to call Kanchan as well. Aunty had not come to work. I got up and went into the kitchen, 'Where is she?'

'She is at home, preparing food for the guests.' Sweety said, and took out case of vegetables. I took it from her and started talking to her.

'Guests!' I exclaimed. She handed me a knife. I was feeling like I was a chef and she was a helper.

'Yeah! Guests,' she said pulling out the canister of flour. She poured the flour in paraat.

'What type of guests?' I asked.

'For Reenu didi.' Things were still unclear.

'What?' I asked.

'Are you with Kanchan or Reenu? She is not your girlfriend. Guests have arrived for Reenu didi's engagement.'

'So why didn't you tell me properly? Cut the vegetables yourself, I'm not your servant.' I told her and hurled the vegetables on the shelf. I got angry with her behavior.

'Who told you to cut them then?' she yawned.

I took out my mobile phone and searched for *princess*. I gave her a missed call. She gave me a missed call back. I called her.

'Hello Vicky.' Kanchan spoke sweetly. Her voice was sweet as sugar. She always started a conversation by calling my name. I was in love again. Yes, I was deeply in love with Kanchan.

'You could have come here,' I said, with a phone kiss, 'Sweety could have handled your guests.'

'Yeah! But mom sent her saying that I was helpless,' Kanchan muttered. I could hear the noise of vessels.

'I'll fuck your sister if she disrespects me again,' I said.

'And you are disrespecting her. Vicky why don't you leave my sisters alone. Are they doing wrong with you?' she asked. Family is family, who am I?

'Is she everything for you? What about me? Am I nothing for you? If they are more important then go and live free. I am going.' I said.

I was upset and I hung up the call.

She tried me back many times but I didn't respond. I was bunking college, avoiding friends, forgetting last affairs. In addition what was she doing for me? She could say falsely that she loves me more than her family. I hadn't heard these words from her side. She loves me, okay I admit it but how could I believe she really did?

I wanted a fight with Sweety too but there is no likelihood of that happening. If I did, she wouldn't cook for us that evening. She was at the root of my controversy with baby doll. She was committed with Anuj that time, a polytechnic student. Anuj was a good looking boy of seventeen, and here she was, a girl who had played with boys double her age.

I was in my room when my phone rang. 'Namaste aunty, you don't come today?'

'No beta, some guests are here to see Reenu,' she told me. *See Reenu.* Is she a buffalo? 'Is Sweety doing well or shall I send Kanchan too?'

'She doing well aunty, no need to send anyone,' I replied. *No one listening my heartbeats. What if you sent Kanchan on her own? But no, you also like my ass to kick.*

'This thirtieth is the date that has been fixed for Reenu's marriage. I wanted to inform you first.' She joyfully said. *Why are you telling me this, tell it to Shiv. I don't care a bit for her.* Aunty was telling this to me and the feelings inside me were like Reenu's brother. Shit!

'Good. It's very close, no?' I asked.

'Yes beta, but why delay when it's been fixed?' I think she was in a hurry to fix the marriage because of some internal problems that she didn't want to share with me. 'Okay beta I have to inform others. I'm sending Kanchan to help her.'

It set me thinking. *Reenu had been with Shiv for the last one year. She must be pregnant. Yes, I am sure she was.*

Kanchan arrived after five minutes. I did not respond to her knocks on my door. Then Hritik called me outside. I knew what she must have said to him: *'Hritik bro, please call Vicky for me once.'*

'You come in if you wish,' I said. Everyone was busy in their work. Hritik knocked at the door and went away. The door was open.

Kanchan entered my room and gave me a sweet glance. 'I'm sorry Vicky,' she said.

'You care for only your family, no? Who I am for you? You shunning me for them, I love you.' I was serious and a tear rolled down from my left eye. She sat near to me on the carpet and wiped it.

'I do care about you Vicky. All are important to me, you as well. I love you too. I can do everything for you, but I need to do things with my family too. You are more precious than anything in my life.' She was just looking into my eyes and wiping my tears. I stood up. 'Where you going Vicky? I am here for you only. Please don't go,' she said and stood up as well, trying to catch my hand again.

'Go. And don't try to call me again,' I said.

18

I tried myself to keep busy in college after that day's conversation. Twenty-one students including five chicks were in my class. I always used to sit with Veer and Aman, who was from Delhi. He had a problem whenever he used to speak vulgarly - everyone kept silent. That day, the class was busy cramming. A friend poked Aman from behind. And Aman said Bhosdi kay!. The Electrical Engineering teacher Jitender sir, was writing on the blackboard. 'Who spoke?' he shouted. All eyes were on our bench except Jitender sir's.

No one responded. The girls were whispering and smiling. Everyone was looking at each other but not naming the person. Unity has strength. Wow! It was amazing.

'I'm gonna calling Mr. Prasad,' he said and took out his phone. Hamid Prasad sir is our HOD. A person without subtitles, who always saw bad things in good people. A moment before Johnny Depp, and next moment Tom Cruise. The expressions on his face were the opposite of what he thought. Aman got strict after that day's incident and our enjoyment was postponed for a few days.

Everybody around me was talking and laughing I was still thinking of Kanchan. I took out my mobile for fiftieth time to check for her missed call but today there was none. My heart sank and it was hard to study the whole day. I was unable to concentrate in my books and on the blackboard.

Bad thoughts were vibrating through my body: *she forgot me. She is in love with another guy. Is she talking with Reenu's husband?*

She'd be busy with the marriage preparations. I have to call her once. She loves you Vicky, remember what she said yesterday. She is a good girl. Good thoughts were in favor. I finally decided to bunk the next lecture. But luckily, the professor did not come. I stepped out of the class and dialed *princess.*

'Hi Vicky. Sorry I was busy at work today. Where are you?' her voice made my eyes wet. I kept my handkerchief on my wet eyes. She was a love goddess. She was behaving like nothing happened between us. I was lucky that she was still with me. I was trying to keep her away from her family. What a dump I was?

'Will you forgive me?' I stupidly asked. I didn't tell her sorry at once and was expecting forgiveness.

'Forgive you for what? You are my sweety and there is no need for forgiveness. And where are you?' She gave me a phone kiss and I heard her mom call for her. 'You are in college, no? Ok Vicky, I'll catch you later. I've to do a lot of stuff.'

'Yes, Ok. Do it. Bye,' I said happily. Now my heart was feeling fresh. I thanked God for sending Kanchan on earth only for me.

'Thank you Vicky,' she said. .

'For what? For all these days when I behaved like shit or to make your life the worst at all,' I finally accepted my offence.

'For calling me, plus yes, I was waiting for your phone call,' she said happily. 'Bye. Love you. Take care.'

'Love you too. Ummmaaaahhhhh.' I gave her a long kiss. Sangeeta, my classmate, was staring at me. She passed me with a smile. She was committed to Kuldeep Solanki, my classmate. He was a school teacher type person. Big number specs, talking manners were legendary. Hair style like a British pop singer. Sangeeta was a rich girl with poor personality. No sense of clothing and makeup. In the name of fashion, a long braid with rusty hair band. Salwar kameez of mismatched colors with slippers. And a handbag of white color torn at many places. There was no sign of an engineering student in her personality.. 'How are you?' I asked her.

'Good. Girlfriend?' she asked, with a sweet grin. She looked stunning after all that day. She had taken a bath that day, I thought. She used a natural lip color.

'Why? If Solanki can have a girlfriend why not me?' I smiled. I wanted to gag on her bag but couldn't.

'I was asking just for information.' She made a face. That was called stupidity. I created another problem for a girl who was the best in class. She was my first friend who was a girl. She moved towards the lecture hall.

'Sorry!' I followed and whispered in her right ear. I was two inches from her and as she turned her face, my lips touched her hair. I almost kissed her cheek.

'What were you doing?' she stared turned around and punched her fist on my chest. Thank God no one was there otherwise the situation could be the cause of a breakup.

'Sorry yaar, yes I have a girlfriend,' I said.

'Whatever,' she said and left with worry lines on her forehead. I was standing in the gallery.

19

After the second semester two members increased in our temporary family. Mussa, Hritik's cousin brother, Sumit Bihari boys' cousin brother. Aunty forced us to feed them on more rates. But we cut it from corner. Reenu had gone after marriage. That day I saw my beautiful cutie in red Lahanga, she was bright as crucially striking princess.

We decided to change our room after second semester. New room was little far for it but good looking too. Days were on track, with no limitations. I was still with Kanchan, and she became my first long term girlfriend. Smriti remained for seven months and Paramjeet for five. A day when Sweety and Kanchan were cooking for us at new room. I was busy in talking with Sweety.

'So, what about Anuj?' I asked in between our discussion. I rarely talked with her when Kanchan came across. And that day I waited for Kanchan's kiss.

'I'm no longer with him, now another boy from same college.' She said as boyfriend manufacturing company chose her new brand ambassador. I tempered again. She was with new boyfriend again. What the rubbish?

'You are with new boy? Means you cheated again?' I asked with red face. She must know my conduct. I wanted to slap her but controlled. Kanchan anticipated my words as well as behavior. She had already awakened by my nature.

'Vicky, come to me please. I have something for you.' She grinned. I was still looking in Sweety's eyes but she'd not make a contact. 'Vicky!'Kanchan shouted on me as my sight turned to her.

'What?' I shouted too. Kanchan signed her to go outside. I curved my body toward her however Kanchan caught my hand and pulled. I straightly fell on her; she adjusted herself and me too.

'Why you asking her silly questions?'Kanchan asked when Sweety left kitchen.

'I asked silly question! Are you mad that taking her favor? What do you really mean by silly queries?' I attacked on her. My full temper dropped on my doll.

'Yes. Is any matter for you here? What if she makes boyfriends?'

'You are saying these words Kanchan? You? I was expecting that you should take my favor in this issue.' I surprised.

'Why? Why should I take your favor?'

'Because I'm right. Look at her, her age, her maturity and behavior. She is looking matured than you do. What is different between you, you know? I do.' I lauded my sound. Fortunately all were absent.

'What?' she asked with eyebrow dance.

'You have a boyfriend since last one year and she changed three. This is not serious?' I answered and questioned.

'Okay! So what you need to ask her about them? You are mine so ordered me not to her. She is nothing for you. I don't care what she does and you have to do same.' She shouted too now.

'I cannot. I am not of your type.'

'Type? What is my type? I am with you, I don't know why she doing it?'Kanchan was looking heavy on me.

'Then you must be same as she does.' I calmed with harsh glare.

'Yes.' She gave me apparent reply. I forcibly punched on wall with full anger in eyes. She frightened furthermore stared in my eyes. She was calm too later this step. She tried to seize my broken hand in her but I drag before her commotion. 'Vicky am sorry.' I left kitchen with shattered hand. My room was just next to kitchen. I entered and shut it inside. She tapped it hardly but I didn't open. She felt apologetic after her deed.

I cried a lot that day. Not for her but for her effort. She was taking her sister's errand in wrong way. I was feeling myself totally unaccompanied. Yes of course she loved me but not more than her sister. On my gaffe I regretted myself, but today I was accurate. I just only tried to make her convince that she could make understand Sweety not to toil like that. I listened some erect noise outside the room. Kanchan was fuming on her sweet sister. *Sweety* no relation with name and functions as well as character too.

20

It was my third semester. Data Structure was a subject that was the most difficult. Harmanpreet Kaur was the teacher allotted for it. A ma'am with dirty nails, unwashed hair, unthreaded eyebrows and unclean clothes, she was unwoman and unsimple and unwow. In all her bad things, her smile was good to see. I hated her presence in close proximity to me. She smelt like she ate only pickle with parantha. Her clothes were dirty as her whole body. A dangerous subject handled by a dangerous teacher. But Veer was good in this subject. Ma'am was attracted toward him. Her eyes spoke volumes.

The class knew about them. Veer had already told me about her attraction for him. She was a poor girl without a boyfriend I think. She needed it of course.

We studied but all Veer did was stare her. She was ready to accept his proposal. But he was frightened a bit for being in a relationship with a teacher. Of course, he was not Shahrukh Khan, neither was she Sushmita Sen of *Main Hoon Na.* But rumors attained abounded in college. Sharmila Rana was our computer teacher in the first semester and she was the nicest yet most strict faculty. We were busy in gossiping with Sharmila ma'am and then:

'This is tough ma'am. I cannot handle it,' Veer said once during problem solving. We were in her lab.

'Why would you find it easy - I'm not your Data Structure teacher am I?' Sharmila ma'am taunted. We looked at her. Veer's face became small and colorless.

'What ma'am? What do you mean?' I tried to get Veer into more trouble. We both teased him. He put his foot on mine.

'If this work had been for Harmanpreet ma'am he would have done it,' Ma'am explained.

'Yes ma'am and with full passion too! That is why he attends only DS!' I dropped ghee in the fire.

'Who asked you?' Ma'am cut me. She removed her red framed specs and rolled her eyes. She looked at Veer. She made it personal and threw me out of this all.

'I don't know ma'am,' Veer shrugged his shoulders, raised his eyebrows and hands. He was in trouble here. The issue was that if ma'am knew, then the whole college would. And if the news reached Mr. Prasad, then God knows what the conclusion would be.

'I know beta. Don't worry you must know soon that there is little gap between a slap and the cheek,' Ma'am was in form. She was hitting only boundaries and was not interested in single or double.

'What are you talking about ma'am? I think we have to go,' Veer stood up.

I too got up and left.

'You!' Veer said and ran behind me. He caught me on the stairs and put his arm on me. We then left college together.

21

It was Kanchan's fifth recharge to my number. She thought that if she recharged my SIM, I'd call her to say don't do this. But I was totally angry about that evening's incident. Two days passed and I didn't talk to her. She came, cooked and went. I didn't see her face for three continuous days. She asked Hritik to intervene. He tried to convince me but I didn't listen. You know, I was into her fully, but she was into me, into mother, sister and family.

I got a call from Jolly. 'Hey! Buddy. How's you?'

'Good. What about your sweetheart and you?' I asked. Jolly was my elder brother. We are more than brothers - we are best friends. We share our thoughts as well as all other things. We don't hesitate to tell anything to each other. We wouldn't miss an opportunity to fuck the same girl at one time.

'Fine. Still with Kanchan or is it another chick?' he asked. He was in love with a village girl. She used to smile at him. She is a good looking girl but seven or eight years younger to him. Jolly's agenda is, to prepare a young girl and to wait till she becomes mature. I never understood what he really wanted. He always said that show off a girl as girlfriend and sex with her like a wife. I never followed him.

'Yup!' I said, 'What happened? She kicked you? I told you bro do the job and fuck the boss,' he said. 'Nothing is like that. How's mom anyway?' I asked. 'She is good. Waiting for your calls - why are you not calling her?' he asked. Who said him that his younger bro was in love.

'It's nothing,' I lied. He wanted to know about other things but I was not in the mood to tell him. 'Ok bye. I'll call you later,' I said and hung up.

It was the fourth night without her, I was tired. I needed her. I wanted a dose of kisses from her on my lips, neck, forehead, eyes, cheek and chin.

She came in evening with aunty that day. I greeted aunty from my room. Kanchan came in and tried to cheer me up. But I was not in the mood for fun. I pushed her out and closed the door tight. I wanted her to grab into the room but my ego stopped me. She would be unhappy with my behavior. But who cared about others? I never did.

I sat on the floor and picked up a book that lay there. Its title was 'Discrete Mathematics'. After opening it, I realized that why math was my biggest enemy. Aryabhatta had invented *zero,* of course. He thought that in twentieth century a genius will be born who will have the necessity for it. I was a zero in love, I was a zero in trust and yes, I was the zero who was creating problems for a hundred percent pure girl. I was turning the pages and thinking about the author who had written such a thick book, when suddenly she knocked on my door. 'Open the door Vicky.' Oh! It was aunty. I opened the door, and found her glaring me.

'What's the matter? I heard that you are not eating in the evening.'

'Actually aunty I..... am....' I could not speak. Through the corner of my eyes, I saw Kanchan looking at me and she started twinkling. I looked down.

'If you are my son then you must eat today in my presence,' Aunty glowered at me. *I'm gonna be your son-in-law aunty ji. Don't say only son, it can be harmful for my relationship with your daughter.*

'I'm sorry aunty, but I am not starving,' I said. 'I just came from Ambala and I ate burger and other stuff.' Aunty didn't reply. She moved and got busy with work. I shut the door again. Kanchan was looking me till the door shut completely.

That night, I could hardly sleep.

Early morning Sweety called me. I was sleepy. 'Hello, Vicky, Kanchan is ill, she cannot come today,' Sweety said in her childish voice.

'I'm not a doctor,' I said and dashed the mobile on the carpet. She destroyed my sleep. I got up and moved to the toilet. Hritik was busy in Hanuman Chalisa. The Bihari brothers were snoring in their room. Mussa and Gujjar were fighting for the blanket. I picked up the newspaper and every article in it was looking most boring.

Someone knocked on the main door. I opened it to see aunty with Sweety. I greeted her and she ignored me. *What the hell?*

'Aunty Namaste!' I said again in confusion. Had she not heard me? But I was wrong, she was really ignoring me.

Aunty came out of the kitchen and entered Hritik's room with the morning meal. I was surprised. What was happening? Did Kanchan share everything she did with her family? Did her mother know everything that happened between us? No, she couldn't do that. After all we were living in India not America where every adult child share their love secrets with mom. Here it happens only in Bollywood. My heart started pumping very fast. I was frightened to think about what everything that was happening so easily. My stomach got heavy and I moved towards the toilet a second time this morning. *I really need to call Kanchan right now,* I thought

'Hi Vicky, sorry for that day.' Kanchan said when she took my call.

I called her to ask, 'Do you share everything about us with your family? How can you do that? Are you shameless or are you making me feel shame?' I had only suspense but I attacked her without even listening to a word from her.

'What are you talking about Vicky?' her voice really low. She sounded unwell. Sweety was right. Aunty must have been angry with me since I made her daughter sick.

'Wow! What fabulous acting. Why don't you try in serials?' I mocked her.

'Vicky I am very sick. Please tell me what is really happening with you? You know that I have been vomiting since last night!'

'Why don't you consult a doctor? You must get well soon. Not tell me, do you tell your family everything?' I asked, ignoring her sickness.

'What are you talking about? I really don't understand,' she said loudly.

'Is your mom aware that we are together?' I shrieked.

'What? Are you mad?' she shouted.

'How you dare to call me mad?'

'I'm sorry Vicky, but I vow I have never spoken to her about you. She will kill me if she gets to know.'

'Leave it, you tell me, how you dare you call me mad?' I started *chutiyapanthi.* 'I'm sorry for what I said baby,' she said. 'The feelings in you are dead, I think. I love you Kanchan more than anything,' I told her.

'I love you too Vicky. I swear I don't tell anyone anything. I think Sweety does it.' She said and the head bell blew for Sweety. She could do anything she wanted to. Even she could fly like a superwoman and beat the boys to cheat on her. No matter how many boys had been cheated by her.

'See your conviction is stinking. She is a bitch and now I gonna tell her off in front of your mom,' I yelled.

'No Vicky. No please, she will take my life. Mom will also get at me,' she pleaded.

'You are right on your place. I will tell your mom everything she does in her absence. There is nothing to fear for you.' I tried to explain. 'What if your intention went wrong?' what a vision she had. Eighth failed girl was talking like a professional. 'I'm sorry Kanchan. How are you?' I finally asked her.

'Now I am feeling better. Why don't you come to my home, Vicky, I want to see you,' she said and I hung up.

Aunty and Sweety were busy cooking. I wore a t-shirt and Capris and ran towards Kanchan's house. She was lying in her mother's room. I put my hand on her forehead, it was warm. She sat crossing her legs and stared at me. I kissed her forehead and asked, 'Now okay?' She shook head then kissed me on the neck. I unclothed her and then we had sex for the first time. We both were virgins - yippee!!!!!!

22

Veer's elder brother Satender was getting married. We all were invited. It was November and winter. We drank a lot and slept with bugs.

The incident as narrated by Veer:

We all were dancing to the DJ's music and you all became drunk. I put you all in one bedroom to sleep. I went to sleep too. Shruthi is my bua's nanad's girl. Yeah! She is my distant cousin sister once or twice removed, but who cared. I can marry her, with my family's permission and with full *Band Baja and Baraat.*

She was on a cot with my mami ji. I walked in, all were chattering and I too sat beside them. I was the only man there. 'Hi,' I said as she shook her head in reply. Mami gawked.

'Beta she is not the only one here. We too exist,' Mami ji said when I turned to her. I sat near mami ji. She put her hand on my head and ruffled my hair. My mom, masi and two sisters were in half-sleeping position, but chit-chatting.

'When you do not exist, you are the bone in meat?' I murmured. I think she heard me.

'Ok beta, I'm leaving,' she said. I feel bad after she left.

'You didn't have to do it.' Shruthi spoke her first words after my entry.

'She is fine, I know.' It was eleven in the night. She was comfortable on her *rajai* and I was still in boots.

'It's cold today, take your rajai.' Shruthi said rubbing her hands.

'Yeah! It should be just the thing.' I followed her, took off my shoes, and got into it. The smile spread on her white face. Light from the bulb was dim. I thought that Neeraj my little sister had not slept till. For the rest, mom and masi were snoring while Minakshi didi's open mouth was indicating that she was sleeping very tight.

'You are doing engineering, no?' Shruthi asked the silly question - even she knew it. This was the first step in a long tête-à-tête.

'Ji. And you?' I asked a silly question too. I know that she is doing her B.Sc.

'You know,' she said. Her teeth were bright as her face. She had a very well-shaped body structure.

'So how's the family?' She was living and studying with my bua.

'Fine. What about Poonam?' she asked. I did not have the guts to face that question. She knew it, but how? Who had told her?

'We are not together these days,' I said without making eye contact.

'What?' she raised up her shoulders and hands with a cute smile. I smelt her light, aromatic perfume. She could become the brand ambassador of deodorant companies.

'Do you have a boyfriend?' I asked. She lowered her head. I knew that Shruthi was not of that type.

'No. Never,' she replied.

'Why?' I stupidly queried. *She does not have a boyfriend because she is a boxing champion. Because she doesn't like boys. I think she hesitates to talk with boys.* I thought of many reasons.

'Because my family doesn't allow me to.' This was her answer. In what era was she living? Which family allows their children to enjoy like this? *My papa says, beta go and enjoy with Sharma ji's daughter. Stupidity!*

'Nice. My father is also against it,' I said. Then our chattering took a dangerous turn and we forgot to sleep. It was a dark smoky night when I stood up to relieve myself. Her eyes were drowsy. We didn't want to waste a time by sleeping. I checked time on my phone - it was five thirty almost. I could hear continuous snoring by two sisters (mom and masi). I yawned. We laughed in sleepy humor.

'I think you have to sleep,' she said it for at least the tenth time.

'You too,' I said rubbing my eyes.

'You both,' I heard a voice. *Fuck.* Neeraj was eavesdropping on us. 'This must be early morning and for God's sake stop it. I cannot sleep in the entire racket,' Neeraj said again. I looked into Shruthi's eyes - she was surprised too.

'How much of your discussion is left?' Minakshi didi woke up and was blinking with half-opened eyes. My mom and masi were still sleeping, thank God.

'This is not sun-up, why you walking around?' it was mami ji. Shruthi hid her face in the rajai on mami's entry.

The three people who had spoken were glaring us. I made a face in shyness. Mami uncovered her shawl and draped it on Shruthi. She then lay down next to Shruthi.

'You didn't sleep the whole night?' Mami said and covered her face and then body.

'Shruthi, please shut your mouth. Switch off the light, I cannot sleep in the light too.' Neeraj called out to her. She got up and switched off the light. End of conversation. I got up to go.

'Where you going? Sleep till dawn.' Minakshi didi heard my footsteps and called out.

The news spread in the ladies group like fire in a jungle that morning. Shruthi and I exchanged contact numbers and danced together on the floor. I was mad for her yaar.

I want to marry her. You know what my parents would say, if her parents come with the proposal, then it would be possible to marry her. But I don't think her father would be ready. She is perfect for me *(Veer shows me her photo on his mobile)*. She reminds me of all my affairs. Her simplicity, her lips, her eyes, her clothes and jewels were looking as if they were made only for her. My search is finished yaar. She is the one who I was waiting for.

23

He stopped the narrative and I fell into thoughts of my Shruthi, I mean Kanchan… Our first expression, first kiss and sex and then the controversy. She was everything for me. It was almost one year of our relationship. Her birthday came and I presented her with a beautiful teddy bear. She kissed the bear and me.

It was evening. I was in my room and a neighbor came running. He sat very close to me on my couch. We were sharing our thoughts about the girls in the village. Suddenly he started talking about my in-law's family. He was unaware my connection.

That evening Kanchan came and I pounced on her.

'Who is this Michael Jackson?' I rudely asked in reply to her kiss. I was in the kitchen and she kissed me as usual.

'Who? I… don't…. know.' I got my answer from the expression on her face.

'How many things about you do I have to know from others? I told you before our relationship that I hate liars. This is the fifth time you have lied. Every time you betrayed me, how can I believe in you? Please tell me how many boyfriends you have had before me. It's embarrassing to get to know from others.'

'Vicky he was nothing to me. Yes I know him, but we were never in a relationship ever.' Kanchan stated.

'So why does everyone here know about you both?' I demanded.

'My brother gave him my contact number and he did make calls.' She had worry lines.

'Wow! Your brother is awesome - what a family you have!' I taunted.

'Vicky I'm sorry about it but please don't bring in my family. I don't bring your family into any issue,' her expressions changed in a while.

'Because my family is far better than yours,' I shouted at her.

'Who knows? Look Vicky, why are we bothering about others' gossip? They cannot see us together so they doing this and saying nonsense. Believe me, I am true to you here.' She held my face in her hands.

'Ha ha ha, Kanchan my love they even don't know on our relationship,' I killed her seduction.

'Who is saying this, tell me his name!' she said angrily.

'Why? So that you can tell your mom and she can make a scene?' I said.

'I know who it is! It is that master's son, no? He already got a thrashing from us.' She knew him, which meant there should be something wrong.

'Oh, how did you guess? Now I know you are lying. How many times have you been fucked by others? Are you a slut?' Kanchan surprisingly, glared at me.

'You blaming me for nonsense Vicky. You know it very well - I did it only with you. I was a virgin,' Her voice lowered. 'You didn't do it right Kanchan.' I was crying now.

'I'm sorry sweety, please don't weep. Look in my eyes, Vicky, I do promise. I'll not tell you an untruth ever again. But please forgive me this last time. I love only you Vicky and I cannot think about other guy other than you. Yes I was guilty in not telling you about him, but he was nothing to tell about. Believe me please.' She wiped my tears and hugged me. I know I cannot leave her ever.

'Is anything left?' I grab her waist very tight and she loosed her body. 'No, Nothing,' and finally she seduced me by kissing my cheek. 'I don't want to hear about you from others.'

'Ok. Why you crying like girls? You are a boy and behave like it,' she taunted me.

'Because these days girls are behaving like boys. They eve tease on boys and then put blame on us. Now do your job,' I ordered her to do her work - what she was being paid for. Kanchan gathered the dishes and started to wash them. I went stood behind her and held her stomach. She was bent and her thighs were looking so much bigger than on other days. She said, 'Remember, a few minutes ago, you were calling me *slut*.'

'I am calling you that now too. You are a slut.'

'Then why do you want to fuck me?' she asked and punched her hand smeared with soup on my chest.

'Sluts are used to work like that. I'll pay for it.' I said with a cunning smile.

'So funny,' she said and began to work. Gujjar was busy writing his practicals. Hritik was amending his one question for the fifth time. Mussa was with others playing cards. This was the perfect location as well as time. Kanchan was still busy swabbing. I went close to her. She turned to push me away but before she did, I chewed her upper lip. She yelped, and Gujjar and Hritik glanced into the kitchen.

Kanchan looked at me in anger. She washed her hands and bent down to the slab. I sat down and kissed her till my lips hurt.

She opened her eyes two seconds later. 'You are stupid Vicky. I've to cook for you. Please let me go.' She said in a low voice.

'Not this time. If you will be my wife I will never let you do anything but kiss.' She ran her fingers through my hair. She loved me more than anything. I totally forgot the matter for which I had abused her. After that day I never listen to music by MJ.

24

College time was boring and time pass in the last session. Now only ten or eleven students remained of the original twenty-one. Veer also was mostly absent. That day, when I attended class, only seven were present. Harmanpreet ma'am was busy lecturing.

'Can I come in ma'am?' I asked.

'Where you were till now? Is this the time to come for class?' she asked. She didn't give me permission to go in. But I stepped in. Ma'am shouted again, 'Who gave you permission to enter?'

'Sorry ma'am.' I stepped back as her face turned red.

'Come in,' she then said.

I went in and took my place close to the window. The days were boring as I told you before. Ma'am sat near other guys gossiping. I dialed Veer on my phone.

'Where you are asshole? If you not attending why do you call me then?' I whispered.

'Sorry Bhatti I couldn't wake up in the morning. Where are you now?' He sounded sleepy.

'Where would I be? You put me here, yaar. Never ask me again for college.' I hissed into the phone.

'Okay. What's strength of the class?' he asked.

'Eight including me and the girls.'

'Who are the sisterfuckers?'

'Shubh and Aman.' I told him the names. We never used abuse before college. And when we met the Delhians our tongue got fucked. We only used *motherfuckers.*

'Sorry yaar, Bhatti. Tomorrow hundred percent I'll come,' he said. I knew his promises. Commitment made in the night were always huddled in the quilt in the morning.

'Vikram!' I heard a scream. It was ma'am. 'Get out of my class.' I stood up and left class with the phone to my ear. 'Never attend again,' she shouted and I left class forever.

'I have been thrown out of class by your sweet miss because of you!' I screamed at Veer.

'Who asked you to call me? Put the phone down and let me rest.' He disconnected. Where should I go? I decided to go home. Halfway down the stairs a teacher called out to me. He was our branch teacher Tejbhan Sir.

'Where are you running around Vikram?' he asked.

'Sir I have been thrown out from my class. I was only talking to Veer,' I explained.

'Who threw you out?'

'Harmanpreet ma'am. She hates me sir. I don't know why. I never did any wrong.' I made a childish face.

'These women lecturers are all like this!' he commented. The truth was that every faculty member hated her other than the HOD. So it was plus point for me.

I nodded.

'You know Vikram, not only Harmanpreet, but some others too are of this type.' I understood. Once Tejbhan sir proposed to a ma'am and had she rejected it. Sir thought that it was not a big issue. But the whole college got to know of it. Ladies have a big problem, they cannot digest a thing in their stomachs. And if the matter is that of a senior teacher, then the juniors don't miss a chance. It was very hard for him to digest at all.

'Yes sir I know,' I consoled him..'

'They all are looking busy, no one is taking interest in other activities,' he said and I understood his intention.

'Yes sir, ma'am should have accepted your proposal,' I said slowly.

His face turned red. 'What are you talking about?' he yelled.

'You and the physician,' I said quickly. 'Don't mind sir she has rejected five teachers in three months.'

'What's your problem in this?' he shouted.

'Sorry sir. I think it is good that she rejected you. You deserve a better lady,' I ended. He didn't reply. He turned to go.

'Have a nice evening ahead sir!' I yelled to his back.

25

It was the end of our vacations. We changed our cook. I spent a lot of time speaking to my doll. She called me, recharged my SIM and faced my abuse. In a day of twenty-four hours we talked for ten hours. She fully topped her mobile and mine too with money. It was hard to see my kitchen without her. I couldn't imagine her absence in that place.

I reached Ambala that evening, Hritik was the only one at home. He hugged me tight and said, 'Bhatti I missed you yaar.' Tears fell from his eyes. What? Was he missing me? Why?

'I too,' I lied. I was missing my sweetheart.

'I left her.'

'What? Who?'

'Your sister-in-law.' So that was the matter. He missed me because no one was with him to share his feelings and emotions.

'Why? What are you talking about yaar.' I got serious. *Really I was.*

Narrated by Hritik:

The day mom was in buffalo's crew, father on his work and brother with his gang. Ritika comes with *mom's lahanga.* 'Where is grandma?' she asked.

'No one is here baby, hold my hands and join me,' I romantically caught her thirty-two inches waist. She put the lahangaa on the cot and dodged my hands.

'And Vimal?' she again asked. *Your lips are red. Which lipstick do you use?*

'No.'

'Where is he?' *silky hair. Which shampoo?*

'Don't' know.'

'When is grandma coming?' *Your eyes are almond-shaped. Can I bite them?*

'Don't know.'

'What are you staring for? Fuck me and let me go.' *What? Is she starving only for sex? What the hell?*

'Are you in a hurry? I don't have time for sex. I can only kiss you if you ask.' *Attitude.*

'Go to hell! Are you kidding me? What if I love you - no matter, I'm only an object for sex.' she said jerking.

'Okay baby come to me, I was only kidding.' I grabbed her again. It was hard for my hand to pinion her tight.

'Okay then.' She put her lips on mine and we were lost in heaven.

'You are so sweet jaanu.' I said licking my lips. She opened her lusty almond eyes.

'You too my *Shaktimaan. Love me wildly…'* Was she joking? *Shaktimaan?* My waist is only twenty-five and it is very hard to purchase a pant for this size.

We were roaming with lips locked on the verandah, bedroom and guestroom, etc. She unbuttoned my shirt, my only red shirt, my lucky shirt, my only washed shirt. Ritika could pick me up in that situation. Yes, she was hungry for sex. She was panting and striving to free my precious leather belt. My back was on the cooler and its hook was hurting me but she was unaware of this. Sweat beaded her forehead. Finally she *succeeded* by tearing one belt loop of my one thousand four hundred and fifty rupees Blackberry pant. The next stage was to unbutton it. She did and lowered my pant. Now my Jockey undergarment was visible. It cost me two hundred bucks. Her red eyes were on my lower body and I was helpless, smiling my shame.

'Let's do it. Please, fast… I have a lot of work other than sex.' She was making me a fool. She was there for sex and blaming it on me. I pulled her kurta up but it stuck to her waist. 'What are you doing? You will tear it up. One sec,' she said and pulled. She was the expert.

'Fast I'm dying for you.' I lied to show her that I was hot for her figure. She fully uncovered her top and then *boom…*

'What the hell are you doing?' Vimal shouted.

'What the hell were you doing opening doors?' I asked when Hritik stopped the narrative.. He was really a great *pakaau*. Ritika is an innocent girl who is still bearing him.

'My elder brother complained about it to papa and mom. He has have many girlfriends and fucks everyday a new.' He dropped a tear. I put my right hand on his left shoulder and he hugged me again. *What if my Kanchan sees? She'll think that I am interested in boys. Yuk!*

'It's okay bro calm down and please don't cry.' I gave him sympathy. He rubbed his nose on my only expensive shirt that I used during travels only.

'Papa put my hand on my only niece's head and I promised him that I'll never see Ritika again.' He sobbed and abscond my body.

'It happens yaar I know. Tell me one thing, you didn't sex that day and has been caught without an enjoyment! You both are freaking assholes.' I lessoned. I was expert those days..

'We were ready to do it and he opened the door. I had to satisfy myself with a hand job.' And he started to weep again. 'I love her more than anything *bhai* and cannot live apart from her.'

'Do whatever you want, promises are made to break at the right time.' I said.

'No. I cannot crack my promises. I love my family and my niece is everything for me. What if she gets hurt after I break the swear that I made on her.' He said. I tapped my forehead he could never be.

'Who is telling you to break promises? There is no other way to love everyone at a time. Look at me.' I said and he looked. 'Don't look at me. Look at what I am doing. Look at my work. I promised my family I will say sister to every girl other than my future wife. Am I doing?'

'No. You are a fucking asshole.' He said looking into my eyes.

'So, do what I am doing. First of all you made a big problem by falling in love with your own village girl. And second her brother is a co-worker with your brother. And final and most dangerous is your brother, he is *Prem Chopra.* Celebrate buddy you were lucky, he didn't fuck you both. ' I explained.

He was staring me surprisingly and turned his eyes then said, 'You are right. But what about my niece? I made swear by putting my hand on her head. .'

I stood and went toward bathroom. He followed me. 'What? Want to piss on me?' I said angrily. He stepped back. 'Look bhai…' and he looked at my zip. '…not here. Listen to me carefully. I have an idea, an idea for you and Ritika. Call her and say not to call again on your number.'

'And niece?'

'Oh my God! Why don't you leave the topic for a moment? You are making me mad really.' I said and he lowered down his face. 'Do what I say.'

'But…

'….Niece…shshsh' I stopped him and said.

'No, but Ritika?'

'What?'

'I cannot live without her. She is my life.' He hugged me from behind. I was pissing with both hands on *weapon*.

'What are you doing? Leave me.. I am not saying you to leave her .' I finished and washed my hands.

'Then what? I think you said not to call her or call to me etc' He made childish face.

'I mean… let it go. Do whatever you think.' I stopped my conversation while he followed me..

26

It was hard time for me and Kanchan. She was burning in fury for our parting, I was crying for her love. I called her many times but she did not pick my calls. I was the reason she had left the job as our cook. We were all bored with her menu and I told her to leave her job. I saw Kanchan when she left. She didn't turn back and not give me a look.

A fortnight passed, I didn't see her nor could I speak to her. My face became dirty because of my long beard and mustache. Without her, everything seemed boring. I didn't want to shave because there was no one left for I could do that for. My body started growing fat and ugly. It was not in my hands to control it. Days and nights were passing only within room. Morning and evening walk were just the names.

It was late night, when I got a call from her uncle's mobile.

'Hello,' I said. It was her uncle's number she used to call me from sometimes when there was no balance in her mobile. I wanted to confirm that it was Kanchan or someone else.

'Sorry Vicky,' she said, and a large tear fell down from my eye. Not a single day passed when I didn't cry.

'No baby… I am sorry. Please forgive me,' I said while my throat was not allowing me to speak. I sat in the corner of roof..

'I cannot live without you. But you did wrong Vicky.' Kanchan said.

'I know Kanchan, please forgive me.. I too cannot stay without you.' I kissed the mobile speaker many times. She did the same. We talked for more than one hour that day when suddenly I heard her mother's voice.

'Who are you talking to?'

'No one mom.'

'I know who it can be on your number but with your uncle's phone – it's Vicky, is it not?

'No mommy not Vicky. I swear.' I was hearing their conversation and kept quiet.

'For him, you are betraying me! Who is it then? Hand me the phone,' her mom shouted.

'Mom please why you forcing me? Are you crazy, why should I call him? You don't know what he had done to us?'

'Then, is it another boy? Yes or no?...beep…

I didn't call again. Now I stood and walked downstairs but in the darkness, I fell down and broke my hand, had a leg fractured, my head injured, and heart severed into tiny pieces. I gathered all my ruptured body parts and walked down with one leg. No one to care. If only *Kanchan could come to hold my hand and kiss my whole body by saying. 'Are you okay sweety? Walk carefully baby you not only hurting yourself...'*

Was Kanchan betraying me again? Was she a slut really? Could she be talking to another boy? *No!* Her mom knew about our relationship. Half a month passed and I was missing her because I was in the wrong. And that day she called me and everything me shattered in a while. I had left Navita for Smriti, Smriti for Paramjeet and everything else for Kanchan. And Kanchan gave me, *ghanta!* I was pricking myself, why did I pick up her call? Every night was good because I memorized about her. But the day it was turn on turn and the night passed but I could not sleep..

I decided and remembered a girl named Amandeep Kaur. A very cute and charming baby doll of hardly five feet with a thirty-six inches waist... I was habituated to eating *golgappa's* in those days. Her father owned a handcart from which he sold this stuff. I wanted to forget Kanchan and it was a good idea. You cannot leave anyone easily who you love the most unless the replacement with another one. AK made eye contact and I didn't miss that opportunity.

27

I didn't get a call from Kanchan. I thought she had forgotten me. I started to make advances at Amandeep. One day, when I crossed her cart, she threw me a childish smile. I threw her my mobile number written on a bus ticket. She picked it up and winked at me. *Shocking*!

'Hi!' A word as sweet as her face. She called me for the first time after I gave her my phone number.

'Hello. How's you?' I said.

'Good, what about you? You were looking smart today.' She was buttering me.

'Me? No dear you were looking awesome.' *Have you seen your tummy tiers?*

'Thank you. You know, you are so sweet,' she said.

'You too.' *Have you ever seen a girl fatter than you?*

'Have you a girlfriend?' she asked.

'No. And you?' *Obvious not, I'm just asking for the formalities.*

'No, you are the very first,' she said.

'Oh! That means you are virgin too,' I said stopping myself from making nonsense. Yet I had made nonsense.

'What?' she was shocked now.

'Nothing, do you love me?'

'You tell me first,' she said.

'I do, so I am asking.' I replied.

'I will tell you tomorrow okay?' *Filmy ornament.*

'Okay, I'll wait. I will wish for a yes, *me too.'*

We wasted time for a few more minutes and then disconnected. I remembered Kanchan. My mind flashed back to the days when we were happy with each other.

The morning of the second day, my mobile beeped. It was not Kanchan for sure. 'Hello!' I spoke with closed eyes.

'Good morning.'

'Who's that?'

'Amandeep!'

'Who's Amandeep?'

'Vicky?'

'Yes, but who are you?'

'Amandeep Kaur!'

'Oh..... sorry..... sorry. I was sleepy and I forg...' I hiccupped. When I woke up, I was really terrified.

'I think you forgot me,' she said.

'No, not at all. I was sleeping and in sleep I forget everything. How are you?' I said. I could hear the Hanuman Chalisa, so it should be seven. I usually woke up at eight for college and ten or eleven on holidays. It was a bad morning.

'So I disturbed you!' *no no, it is nice to hear your voice stupid girl.*

'No. So what do you think?' I asked.

She said, 'Yes, I love you.' She laughed. I closed my eyes and put my head down to sleep again.

'Ok then bye, I have to get ready for college.' I hung up and pulled my blanket on my face. *I bunked another day of college day.*

28

Gujjar was snoring, I shook him but he didn't stop. I sat next to him and found that he was sobbing not snoring.

'Gujjar! What happen bro?' I asked. It was rare to see him crying. I noticed a photograph in his hand. *Anjani!* She was his brother's sister-in-law and his love.

He didn't reply. Tears were in his eyes.

'Is everything okay, tell me yaar!' I said, '…and why are you not in college?'

'His family has fixed her wedding,' he replied in a sobbing voice. 'I love her yaar, but my family…. Papa will never agree.'

'When did you know?' I put my hand on his shoulder and he hugged me. I cannot explain what happened to me, I had probably wept as well.

'This morning,' he said.

'Stop please. This is hard time I know. But you have to be strong.' I know I am not a good man but I never played with someone's emotions. I felt bad the day when Jeet was kicked by his girlfriend. I felt bad too for Hritik and here I was unhappy. Around me, the world was unique but I was unaware. One by one my all friends were facing the same crisis. I thought about Kanchan at that moment. It was around one and half months that we were apart.

'She is everything for me you know and we were happy together. She never demanded gift items like other's girlfriends do. She gave me many gifts on my b'days and other occasions. The morning was not good for both of us. I don't cry for anyone and anything but today she was crying. She is against this marriage.' He was continuously crying and talking and I was listening to him carefully. In between, he wiped his tears and nose many times. I consoled him but thoughts were different: *then why you telling it to me. My condition is also same as you. Even you girlfriend crying but mine has no emotions. Mr. Gujjar calm down and try on another girl like I do.* When he stopped I said, 'Okay, I understood now, please stand up and wash your face.'

'No I am okay you go,' he said as he got my meaning.

I was not trying to concentrate on brushing the truth but my friends' worst faces were stopping me from doing the same. Jeet, Hritik and now Gujjar, I saw and consoled every one of them. Jeet was no more interested in girls. Hritik was forgetting Ritika by concentrating on *Structural Analysis, Mathematics and Building Construction* subject. Despite all the heartbreak around me, I had never lost my interest from girls and never took any interest in books. Amandeep was filling her place but emptiness was still in my heart, and it was eating me inside like white ants. Kanchan was not calling me but somewhere in my heart I was missing her. I couldn't bear it anymore. I was in need of her.

29

I tried to forget Kanchan totally but in vain. I was gasping for her and she was ignorant of it. It didn't matter until one day Amandeep called when she was alone at her home. I refused her on her first call but later she forced me. I returned from college before lunch. I checked that the street was empty and entered. She was in her room. The front was a dry grass lawn filled with feathers and leaves. Distemper was torn up from walls and gates, a handcart at the other corner. She lowered her eyes after a sugary glance. I caught her arm and pushed her inside. She didn't react, which meant that she was ready. She was hugging me tightly..

'Where are your family members?' I mumbled into her ear.

'No one is here,' She was breathing heavily. Her hands were around me.

'So?'

'Ambala!' she opened her eyes at my rude manners.

I hold her long waist and pushed her down on the bed. She was acting helpless. I showered kisses on her face and lips. I did this for two or three minutes but my body was still cold. I stood and looked into her closed eyes.

'I'm sorry.' I said and adjusted my t-shirt.

'What happened?' she smoothed her hair and then her kurta. She appeared surprised.

Kanchan was not only in my breath but she was in my body, in my spirit. Amandeep held my hand and kissed me on my neck. Yes! I closed my eyes and then we lost in a dust of dirty deeds. I did everything without telling a word. She changed her clothes and I left her home. When a girl gives her body to a boy, her worship becomes incredible. Amandeep was also a girl of that category. She started calling me a hundred times in a single day. She was now the second girl recharging my cell number without any reason. Ten days passed and we enjoyed our time together.

One day, Kanchan's little brother handed me a letter. I opened it very fast and the very first word I read wetted my eyes. How could I do that to her? What had I done with such a sweet girl?

Sorry sorry sorry Vicky.

I am sorry Vicky, I am not calling you. You know the reason very well please forgive me. In the next two or three days I am purchasing a new mobile with my own money. I know you have missed me so much. The last day, when we talked, mom caught me red-handed. I didn't call you these hard days so that mom could forget about us and she did. Now we both will be together again forever.

I know it to be hard time for you. I was tense thinking about you all the time. I cannot explain how much I missed you, your kisses, your bites. I have been trying to write you for the last few days, I was thinking I was a fool. Everything what you did to make me laugh, thanks. You remain in my brain, soul, body and heart. I feel grateful to God that he sent you into my dull and dreary life, to change my lifestyle, my routine and my heart towards guys. In my sight, guys were only famished for sex but your willpower proved it that you not.

She was fabulous in love, awesome in kissing and tremendous in sex. She made me to feel like a superstar. I was crying. I began to read again:

Today evening I am coming to see you giving mommy another excuse. I want to see you and you have to be there otherwise the result will be harmful. You know I am a GAWAAR type of girl so forget my mistakes and accept my huge love only made for you. I love you so much. Bye!.

Your Kanchan forever

A kiss in brown lipstick' signed off her name. I read it twice, thrice and kept the letter in carefully in my bag. I went to the terrace to wait.

Kanchan appeared with Sweety. They were both staring at me. Kanchan was in a peacock blue kurta-salwar with a blue and white dupatta. She raised her eyes and smiled. I was only looking at her face. It was one and half months since I saw her the last time. Her catwalk, hair clips, foot wears and everything I was just wanting to see her one sight. I saw her until she blurred. I was stunned to see her look so beautiful. I then came down and she returned when I didn't know. The day after I got a call from her, and she invited me to her home. Her mom had an appointment. I went direct to her ammi's room, when a super shocking surprise was waiting for me. Kanchan, Sweety, a friend and Amandeep - those four turned their eyes toward me. My face turned yellow.

A girl who was common friends with both Kanchan and Amandeep had ratted. I looked at Kanchan, then at Amandeep. Amandeep wept. Kanchan glared. Sweety and the *friend* left the room. Amandeep raised her steps and my body got small in shame.

'Why Vicky?' Amandeep asked. I lowered my head. 'Look into my eyes! Why?' and she shouted weeping.

'I'm sorry,' I said. As soon my words came out, her palm landed on my cheek. *It was my first slap from a girl.*

Then Kanchan came near and I expected her to slap me but, 'I thought you are dying for me. But what do you do with my feelings? Is she so sweet or she has a different pussy.? The only difference is that she has big boobs. But can she love you more than I do? Vicky I waited for you. I was spending my time thinking of you. I could have slept with any boy in your absence but I couldn't… why? I loved you goddamn.'

Loved…

The word shook me fully inside and outside. *Is she leaving me? Will she go and get married at her mom's will?*

'Go!' she said. She was furious.

'Listen to me, Kanchan. I love…'

'Oh! Please! Don't waste your time in these formalities. You showed what you really are!'

'I was needy. You were not calling me. I needed someone to hold my hand,' I tried to explain.

'And me? What about me, I was not needy? Have I not a heart? I was burning too. I could make boyfriends, have sex. But I didn't do that Vicky. 'cause I loved you. I really loved you. I never thought about other boys after you. Now please go, my mom is coming,' she said.

I tried to hold her hand, 'Kanchan….'

'Don't ever touch me!' she pulled away her hand.

'I'm sorry, I have just a sentence to say to you, nothing more.'

'Leave!'

I came out of the room. Sweety and the friend were there, smiling. The friend was sexy, looking hot with thin a waist and thick buttocks. She was tall. I thought, *why she is not my girlfriend? I can satisfy her.* I can bet she was not virgin.

'Go Vicky, here is nothing left for you.' Suddenly, I heard Kanchan again. I stepped out of the home and Kanchan was shouting at other girls.

The session ended and we all friends left for our respective homes.

30

Before noon I got a call. Kanchan did not call me after that. *It was* Hritik!

'Your brother is committing suicide bro,' his drunken voice on the phone! *What the hell!* He never said like that.

'What!'

'Yupe,' he said.

'But why!' I screamed.

'You tell, why not?'

'How can I say?'

'She is going.'

'Who?'

'She! You don't know?'

'But who is she? No I don't.'

'Your Bhabhi.'

'Ritika?'

'Who else is your Bhabhi?'

'Where?'

'She is getting married.'

'To whom?'

'What is the matter? She is going, just don't worry.' I woke up fully now, stood and went to the toilet. He continued, 'After five months I cannot see her go. Let me come to your place. Send your proper address to me.'

'Okay I will. And you are drunk in the morning, it's tea time.' I screamed at him, showing him brotherhood.

'No brother, check your watch it is drink time.' I checked, it was nearly eleven. No one had woke me up.

'No! I think I will not come to your home – what will your family think? I'll go to Ambala,' he said. My mobile beeped for another call. *Oh my God! Kanchan! She has called me finally.* 'Papa is saying stay but I cannot see her go yaar…'

'I'll catch you later…' I said.

'Why? You are only my brother and you are not talking to me.'

'Kanchan is calling.'

'You are ignoring me for a useless girl,' he said. I know he was not in his senses or else he would never have used such words for her.

'Don't forget, she calls you *Brother*,' I corrected him.

'I know but this word is only for *girls* not for Kanchan. Please yaar, you can call her later but I may not call you after today.' He was indicating suicide. So he talked and Kanchan kept calling. Twenty minutes passed and he gave up finally.

7 missed calls.

I dialed as soon as I could. She picked up.

'Hello!' Kanchan said.

'I knew you would call me Kanchan.' I said. I still was in my room.

'You were busy?' she screamed. After a long time, her screaming voice sounded good to my ears.

'Hritik! You forgive me baby?' I asked.

'No! Was it moti?'

'No! It was Hritik. He is upset, so he made a call. I swear, Kanchan believe me.'

'So long! How can he talk for so long? I don't believe you.'

'So you called me up get to know if I am alive or not?'

'Like….' she said but I stopped her.

'Then you can leave me,' I said and she calmed down.

'I called you just to tell you that I slapped her.'

'Who?' I asked.

'Your moti,' she taunted.

'What? Did you really slap her? No!' I astonishingly felt happy. *Kanchan slapped Amandeep! How can a fly kill an elephant? I didn't believe it easily.*

'How could she dare touch you?' thank God she didn't know that Amandeep had slept with me too otherwise she would kill her.

'And?' I asked further.

'And what? She apologized for what she had done. I then forgave her,' she explained.

'And are you not forgiving me? Is she special to you more than me?'

'I forgave you that day.'

'Then why have you not called me all these days?'

'Because I wanted to concentrate on my work but…'

'But?'

'…. I couldn't. Your memories keep disturbing me. I am sorry to leave you alone'

'I am sorry baby. But I never forgot you.'

'I know, your mouth can speak lie but your voice and face cannot. Amandeep told me that you love only me…' she kept talking.

Amandeep told her that I love only Kanchan, Kanchan slapped Amandeep and Amandeep apologized for what she had done. So Amandeep hadn't told her about our sex life. She didn't tell because she thinks… What does she think? I have to call her otherwise I would never be free.

'Kanchan, I will call later?' I said.

'No!' she yelled.

'Please baby! I just remembered an important work, please let me go. I will call you. Sure!' I mollified her and she agreed.

'Go to hell! Don't ever try to call me.' Yes she agreed of course. 'Thank you baby love you bye.' I disconnected. I convinced a girl to make a call to another girl. How disgusting was I?

I used grandpa's phone to make a call. She picked up, a sweet injured voice. 'Hello who's that?'

'Amandeep!' I said little slowly.

'Who? Vicky?' She recognized me yippee!

'Hi!'

'Why do you call me?' she asked. *Why does a handsome boy call a beautiful girl? Err!*

'Thank you. Thank you very much and sorry for what I had done. You really deserved a good partner that I could never be that.'

'Say thanks to your girlfriend,' she confused me now.

'For what?' I mumbled.

'You don't know?' she asked. 'You really don't know?' she frightened me.

'What don't know? What do you mean?' I was tense.

'Okay!'

Then she narrates:

Kanchan came one late evening to my home. I was still sobbing. Mom had asked many times what the problem was but I didn't tell her anything.

'Sorry,' she said and sat close to me. 'You know, who Vicky really is?' she held my hand. I didn't reply. She touched me with her fingers. 'I am touching you because he did. He called me and said, say sorry to Amandeep for me. He couldn't face you. He loves me and before everything happened, in some way I was at fault. I let him go for a long time. Boys cannot handle this period. Forgive him.'

'You still love him?' I wiped my tears.

'How can I forget him? He taught me the real definition of love. Yes, I love him,' she assertively said.

'He loves only you.' I said and she left.

'She really loves you.'

'Yeah I know,' I said. Amandeep was good for me, she gave me her *ijjat,* and she showed no arrogance. *I must say that if Kanchan dropped me, I wanted to be caught only by her.*

'And me? What was my fault but to love you?' she quivered. *How could I forget that she was also a girl?*

'I….I am sorry,' I murmured.

'You just say sorry and I forget? It is not so straightforward Vicky. You think that if you betrayed someone, God will do nothing? You cannot get her ever! I curse you!' she shrieked.

I cut the line. Grandma called for lunch. She didn't know that my stomach was already full with abuses. I was replacing myself from one cot to another like bugs were eating my ass. Kanchan was a good girl with a clean heart, Amandeep a good girl with an unclean heart, Vicky was a bad boy with a black heart. Kanchan was smiling in a photo that I captured at her home. I was staring into her eyes.

31

'Can we talk if you are not busy?' Papa said to me one day looking serious. I am reminded of all the sins I had ever made. There was something wrong in his words.

'Yeah!' I could say only that.

'Whom with were you busy with on the phone late last night? Will you please explain?' Papa tried to be a father. I had been trapped obviously. I had no more lies to hide from him.

But I tried a few. 'No one paa!' I made a face.

'You think I am a fool. And if you really think that then don't forget I'm your father too. You will never say *baby* to your mom, no? That should be a young girl.'

We were talking late night, that should be midnight I guess. But where was papa? *Fuck*! We then made phone sex too. I was speechless.

'Classmate?' Papa asked.

'No!' *I'm not so lucky papa.*

'College-mate?' Papa asked again.

'No!' *those all have boyfriends and your son is not Brad Pitt.*

'Then?' Now it was his turn to be surprised.

'A girl.....' I was almost near the word.

'Yes I know a girl...' *my son is not Brad Pitt but can't be a gay too, maybe papa thought. Because there was his respect on pointy edge.*

'My cook!' I said finally.

'Cook!' Papa screamed. His son was doing engineering and had fallen in love with the cook! He was expecting an educated *bahu.*

'No! She is her daughter!' I explained.

'Whatever? She is your cook, is that not enough?' Papa howled. 'And you gonna marry her?'

'No paa! Of course not!'

'And never think about it,' Papa said and moved.

I had never thought of getting married to Kanchan. We kissed, we missed, we loved and we did sex. She had never asked me to be her life partner. But she behaved like a wife. Once I gifted her a ring of rupees ten that I had bought from the village fair. She never wore it on her finger but kept it in her bag. I asked for the reason but she only said that she didn't want to lose such a precious gift at any cost. The poor lady didn't know the real price and if she did, she would have thrown it into the bin. And obviously, I didn't tell.

Kanchan's phone!

'Hello!' I said with a wrinkled face.

'How was the night?' she asked.

'Screwed and yours?' I asked.

'Fun! What happened?'

'Papa caught us,' I told her.

'So what? Tell papa I was talking with your bahu,' she laughed.

'It's not funny Kanchan,' I screeched. 'My family is not like yours. He will kill me you know.'

'What do you mean by my family?' She was sounding angry now.

'Hey! I didn't mean it. I only wanted to say that my family will never allow me…'

'And my family? Disgusting!' she shrieked and hung up.

'Listen…' She had hung up.

I dialed back but couldn't get through. I meant that *my family is old-fashioned, not modern like yours.* But she jumped to a conclusion herself.

Jolly was trying to hit on our village girl. He had no time for me and my affairs. The girl belonged to a low caste. My brother is two years and eighteen days older to me but looks younger. I told him my problem about Kanchan and he said, *'Look here are many beautiful asses in our village why you running after her. You know that a village girl can satisfy you after her marriage too. Will Kanchan sleep with you after the wedding or will you travel three and twenty hundred milestones for her after your Btech? No! Then do whatever I do and life will suck your penis.'*

He and his dictums always disturbed me. When his girl went for exams he followed her to help her cheat. She passed him smiles and he again followed her. Five thousand bucks fuel he wasted on her. I said, *'If you paid such an amount on G.B. Road, you could get five chicks more fabulous than her.'* He said, *'She is your bhabhi, mind your language and brain. And anyway there is a word something like virgin, do you know?'* and he laughed, while I became jealous.

I had no way to soothe myself. She had not been taking my calls. I tried Sweety's phone but she was busy. Yes, she had changed her boyfriend again. I forget the exact count but this time I didn't interfere. Actually Kanchan had told me not to interfere in Sweety's life. And I didn't want to spoil my second anniversary too.

Then Veer called. Veer *the lover boy* was sobbing on the other side.

32

'Viru!' I exclaimed. My friend was broken up. Apparently he had also been kicked by a girl. The lion-hearted boy crying like a baby.

He said 'Shruthi is no more with me Bhatti. Now I can understand how girls had felt after I left them.'

'Yaar what is happening with all us?' I became nervous. Veer was just near the final step with her. Even his kin had allowed him to marry her. I thought that he would be the only one among us to marry the girl he loved. 'What exactly happened?'

'She blames me for everything. Now she is talking of my previous affairs. Did she not know before? Disgusting!' He was angry.

'So this one is gone you think?' I asked.

'Maybe! Actually her mom picked up my phone and she abused me, 'Don't call here again.' Then Shruthi called me back and fought with me. But this is an old incident,' he explained.

'Old incident! Then what is the latest?'

'She broke up!' he exclaimed, 'now she wants to separate. Her mom censured me and complained to bua. And bua was also angry with me saying what I need to call her if she is not interested anymore. What do I do now, I cannot leave her...?'

'Bua is right. Why were you calling her if she didn't want to speak to you? Look she is a good girl and maybe she is under pressure,' I suggested.

'She can tell me that, can't she? I think I have to change my ways,' he said.

'It would be better for both of you,' I said.

'Yeah! The only way to keep myself happy and quiet,' he wept again.

'So why did you call me?'

'Only you can understand your bro's feelings. Only you will not make a joke of my feelings. I feel better now yaar. She made me cry for three days. I couldn't sleep properly, eat, laugh or talk. I'll never call her again.'

'Is she faulty that you think?''I don't know and don't care anyway.'

'You have to. My sixth sense says that she did it only for you, for peace in family. Yes! She still loves you, I am sure,' I told him.

'I've to go yaar. Thanks!'

'Anytime.'

Veer was like my elder brother. And I cared about him. I was sad because he was crying. He was apart from all Jaats, he had faith, love, understanding and more importantly, emotions. And I could feel his emotions.

Classes had started and Kanchan was also talking to me.

Her mom knew but was helpless. She sent many agents to me to threaten that I would stay away from her daughter. But I told her to tell her daughter to stop first, then I would. Mom beat up her young daughter then.

Once Kanchan's mom beat her with plastic pipe and of course, I was the cause of her beating. She was happy and felt herself lucky. She thought that people are rare who get hurt by family in love. Poor lady! If my papa beat me like she did, I would either have committed suicide or run from the house. I cried for her blind love, I cried because she owed me and I cried because I did care about her.

Of course, she was happy that day too but I could hear a pain in her voice. She was poorly sick of love indeed. I was too much far from her. I could not hug her, I could not kiss her and I could not see her. I was missing her like never before. Kanchan was mad for me, her mom was mad because of me and I was mad because Kanchan and her mom were mad. *Confusing!* Anyway I finally decided to attend classes after one month.

I checked my phone – there were five missed calls from a number. I called the number.

'Vicky, will you marry Kanchan?' it was aunty. *Fuck!* It was too late. Missed calls were made by Kanchan but I was too late now. I was silent. She asked again.

'Aunty, I don't know.' I murmured.

'Then please stop calling her. I don't want you to rot you in jail. You are a good boy I like you but only if you love my daughter and marry her. Say yes and make her your own otherwise leave her for me.' Aunty said and waited for my reply. I paused and she hung up.

33

I decided that night to change my life. I wanted to celebrate that moment. I told Hritik to bring wine for all out buddies. All were happy in my celebration except for me. I was happy for Kanchan.

'Is it?' Gujjar barked, as I turned my face towards him. One hand was on the bottle and the other, on the snacks.

'What do you mean?' I hiccupped. Yes I knew, he was demanding more wine. I gave five hundred bucks and one left to take another bottle of a different brand. The phone beeped - it was Kanchan. I took her call.

'Hi Vicky!' she said as usual.

'Hi how's you?' my voice was not steady.

'You are drunk?' her voice sounded gloomy.

'So what?' I said.

'Vicky, are you drinking?'

'Yes. So?'

'Unbelievable! Why? Are you mad? You promised me that you'll never touch wine!' she exclaimed.

'Ummmmmm, I forgot!' I simply said.

'Forgot! How can you say it so simply? Is this about me?'

'What about you? Why do you take all on yourself?'

'Then what is it Vicky, why don't you tell me? Is it a secret that you don't want to share?' she asked as Gujjar called me back to sit. 'I knew all are drinkers… but you!'

'Can you meet me? It's urgent,' I said.

'Like this, never. You are a freak and I don't wanna meet you in this condition,' she exclaimed.

'You call me *freak?'* I said.

'No, I mean we cannot meet right now.'

'Yes you said,' I shouted.

'Vicky how can I say you freak? I wanted to say that…'

'You call me *freak* again. How you dare to talk with me like this?' I made *chutiyapanthi.*

'Vicky I was trying you to understand that…'

'What understand? You think I'm a fool?' I tighten my voice.

'I'm sorry Vicky if I said you anything unintentionally,' she was on her feet now.

'Are you are ignoring me? Yes I am noticing it these few days. Your phone is also engaged when I call you. You are letting me go, no?'

'No, never Vicky. How can I leave you, you are everything to me. I am sorry, but please don't accuse me. I have loved only one person in my life.' She was probably crying but I was so drunk that I didn't care about it at all.

'You loved! Yes you loved, Kanchan. You loved only one person that was me, but not now. You said so yourself.' I continued, 'If you think that I am nobody now, then release me, leave me. I don't want a relationship with a girl who behaves with double standards. This time, let's pack up.' I said as effortlessly as I had said *I love you.*

'You decide this yourself. You didn't think about me a bit, my feelings or emotions. You can live without me, but I cannot live without you. I will never let you go. I will call you back when you are sober,' she said and hung up. I caught the wall to try support my body but couldn't and fell.

'Cut off! *Saali!*' I mumbled, lying on the floor. I slept that night on the bare ground. This is what drinkers do daily. Early next morning my head felt totally hammered. I felt like a huge mountain was kept on my head. I had drunk three pegs without water. My mouth tasted like hell. I drank two glassed of water that morning. I checked for my mobile but it was not there. I searched for it and got it. When I picked it up it was vibrating *Kanchan*! I disconnected the call and went to the toilet.

OMG! There were seventy missed calls! I was shocked. She tried my number continuously till I switched it off. I am sure she didn't sleep that night. I went to college that day for the third lecture. It was hard to keep mobile off for the full day. I bunked college at lunch time and switched on my cell phone. As I expected, in a while I got her call.

I have to attend it one last time I whispered myself. The reality is that I cannot exist without her.

'*Vicky please!* Hello! Vicky, why are you not taking my calls? And what happened to your phone? Please don't stop calling me. Okay? You understand?'

'I told you last night, don't call me. Do you remember?' I screamed.

'No I cannot,' she howled. 'Vicky I want to see you - please come to my home. I am alone here. Mom has an appointment with the doctor and all are out. Please come here one last time,' she said. She thought she could placate me. Her feelings and touch always melt me. But today I was not going to play.

'Hold on I am coming if that's your last wish,' I said and ran to her home. In three minutes I reached her main door. It was open. I entered.

The house was a mess. She was in her grandma's bedroom. I entered and she held my waist. I wanted to grab her tight but my dignity stopped me. I wanted to kiss her lips but my God stopped me. I wanted to take off her clothes but my mom had said to me that wear only your clothes. JK!

I caught her shoulders and looked at her. Red eyes, uncombed hair, unthreaded eyebrows and grubby dress. She was wearing my favorite outfit - a black salwar kurta and white dupatta. She was not taking care of herself. I was still staring in her eyes. Which Kanchan I left and which one was there? *Aunty I will kill you.* I shouted inside the my body.

'Vicky please.' She requested.

'It's over. I cannot handle this relationship any further. You are not mine. I loved you but you betrayed me,' I said, crying inside.

'I never think about any other person but you. Not in my dreams even. I am all yours pure and clean,' she said and then requested, 'Please hug me Vicky I need it. You cannot leave me,' she said and struggled to seize my collar. But I stepped back and her hands grabbed only air. A small tear rolled down her white cheek. My heart found relief. Today she proved that she loved me. I wanted to say her that *you are looking gorgeous unwashed too baby. But your tears are damaging your beauty. Now I realize why you don't cry.* But I couldn't say a word. She stood in the same position like a statue. Tears were rolling down.

'I am going Kanchan forever,' I said..

She removed her dupatta and said, 'Do anything with me Vicky. But please don't go. My body is only for you and no other I will destroy myself. Kanchan will die without Vicky,' she said wet-eyed. I hardened my heart but I cannot explain how bad I felt at that moment. She was offering me her dignity with exchange of the love. She was a love *Goddess*.

'Bye,' I said. I left her home, her street, her sentiments and her love. I wanted to say that *Vicky will also die without Kanchan. She is everything for me, and she is the guardian angel that fills my energy, breath, love, courage and belief.* Belief! Yes I believed her and she believed me but what did I give her?

I wanted to cry a lot. Aunty and Sweety would be happy to know that I had broken up with her.

My legs were not bearing my lethal body. One step ahead was pulling me backside. Hundred meter distance turned hundred miles. I went home, lay on my bed, pulled out her photos and kissed them a hundred times.

I drank, I hardly ate and forgot when I ate.

My friends were distressed by my changed behavior. Gujjar tried to stop me forcefully. Hritik tried emotionally and Veer gave his own example. Hritik told my family and papa slapped me for the first time. This was my last year at college, so they couldn't get me home. Mom was angry with her favourite child. She restricted my phone calls. My pocket money decreased from the next month. Hritik paid my room rent.

Bamboo Rest-O-Mania:

Suddenly my phone rang and I took the call, 'Hi... listen Divyanshi, I will catch you later... Ok bye...' Arun was staring at me. 'What?' I asked him.

'Who is she?' Arun asked. We gulped down six beers.

'She?Ah! She is Divyanshi. My girlfriend almost.'

'GF! Which one?'

'One of whom Jolly is unaware,' I smiled.

'Then? Will you tell me, I will not tell anyone? Promise!' he said.

'Okay,' and I started.

34

Papa was not taking my calls. I think papa informed mama ji about my life as well so I left for Delhi on mama ji's call. He wanted a meeting to persuade me but I had a reason to leave. Mama ji was close to me so may be papa thought that he can help me mend. New Delhi is a big city and accidents can take place any time. That happened to me. I was crossing the highway via a footpath when a beautiful chick with dark glasses, wearing a headphone pushed her pink Scooty just between my legs. I fell down. When I opened my eyes, I was in hospital. She had admitted me there - thank God I was safe and feeling good.

'How are you feeling? I'm sorry,' she apologized.

'I'm okay,' I smiled.

'And your leg?' she asked.

'Yeah, it's good.' I said, but was shocked to see my plastered right leg hanging from a hospital pulley.

'I'm sorry, it was my mistake. I was on the wrong side of the road.' She held my hand. I could feel her warmth. She was staring into my eyes. She was a smart and high profile babe, as I noticed her face, makeup, nail color, hairless skin, well-maintained figure, fancy ear and nose rings, smart black gown and black hair band.

'Vicky,' I said. She turned her light brown eyes with black kajal on me. She could kill anyone with a wink. I said again, 'My name.'

'Divyanshi Iyer,' she told me her name.

'Is she South Indian?' Arun asked.

'Yeah,' I replied.

'Sorry I thought you won't cross and I….. you know. It was my fault,' she said again.

'It's okay, that's usual in Delhi but today's my bad luck,' I said and she put her hand on my hand.

Kanchan made it many times. Whenever I got stressed she put her hands on my head. It was hard for both of us. The information could make her fall her sick that I am in hospital. I kicked her and God broke my kick.

'Where are you?' Divyanshi clapped in front of my eyes.

'Try to get up, we are leaving,' she said adjusted her finger in my finger gap and pushed my back with her other hand.

'Are you sure? I don't think I can. Just look at my leg,' I pulled my hand back and stuck my head on the pillow.

'Do you know that this is most expensive hospital in Delhi, in India or Asia… I don't know exactly? But in last five hours, I have paid up fourteen thousand rupees. And for your kind information, my account is now empty. Oh! Wait, one more thing, I called your father with your cell phone and he didn't take the call.' She moved towards the door and came back. 'And your wallet has only five hundred. What the fu…?' I smiled and she shouted, 'You think I'm a bitch who is barking after a Lamborghini.'

'Sorry about that let's walk.' I said. *Lamborghini Gallaedo! Rich people dialogue expensive things.* I heard it only in *Smack That* by Akon.

I could not walk properly until she held my waist and right hand. I put my arm on her shoulder. We were in the Fortis Hospital emergency ward. A fat nurse came with a wheel chair. Divyanshi handled it and rolled me out. 'On this Scooty? Never!' I screamed, when I saw the Scooty.

'Hold on dear, I will drive it,' Divyanshi said.

'I won't ride two-wheeler to Najafgarh. Do you know how many kilometers we have to travel?' I said and paused when I saw her wide open eyes.

'We're not going Najafgarh.' She sounded exhausted.

'Okay then, place me on the footpath. I will adjust,' I said. She supported me to help me get up and then moved the bike. I sat on it both legs one side. She self started the bike, 'Let's move?'

'Hmm.'

'We are going to PG,' she said.

'Hain Ji?' I mumbled.

'Not Hain Ji my PG,' she shrieked. We moved and she was driving fast.

'I cannot afford an air conditioned PG in Delhi.' I shouted so that she could hear.

'I am not deaf,' she shouted in reply.

'What?' I didn't hear her.

'You will stay in my room,' she said and slowed her bike.

'Are gents allowed?' I asked.

'No, but who knows that you are a gent?' she asked.

'What? I think you want proof?'

'I meant that we'll enter late night around closing time. And no one will ask as long as I'm with you.'

'They will identify me no?' I inquired.

'No, they not until you not show them your ID or face,' she was driving fast.

I grabbed her long and slim waist on speed breakers. After two or three kilometers, she stopped and puts the stand. 'Is it?'

'No, let's have some fast food. I'm starving. And you?'

'I'm ok, I probably have to vomit.'

'Yuk! Are you a girl?' she sniffed.

'No I am sick.' And found a safe zone with one leg and vomit. It was my first time when I vomit during travel by a two-wheeler.

'You need doctor again, no?' she advised or asked I don't know.

'No, gas problem may be.'

'How disgusting you are? Why you eat inedible?' she was forcing me to slap her white cheek.

'Will you shut your fucking mouth? I was on an empty stomach when you hit me.' I did more than a slap. She took off her glasses looking at me surprised. Her white face turned whiter. She was looking beautiful after all.

'I'm going to have a coffee,' she said quietly. But I was expecting a slap from her too.

'I would like one too,' I said, apologetically.

We kept silent and I sipped with a long *shuuurrrrrr.* She smiled with closed lips and turned her face. I sipped again and this time with no sound.

'I'm sorry,' I said staring at the coffee mug. 'The taste is strange of this coffee. I think they forgot to boil it.' I stupidly said.

'Cold coffee,' she smiled again but this time with glittering teeth.

'Oh!' for the very first time I tasted cold coffee. It was really strange for me. She finished her cup and I was still looking at the flower in my cup. I have to choose the tea. *I was confused, because the cup size was extra large and second how they create a flower in the coffee.*

'You can leave if you don't like it,' she paid for both 'keep the change'.

'Wow! I saw the first person who said those words other than movies. In Haryana Roadways, the bus conductor gives candies to avoid change issues.

'How much do I have to pay?' I asked.

'For what?' she asked and kept her wallet in her bag.

'Coffee.' I said.

'Why?'

'I will return you whenever I come here.' I supported the wall,

'You are not looking *chutiya* as you trying to be. It's the first time that I'm paying when a boy is with me. So enjoy whatever I do for you,' she covered her head with the helmet.

She helped me onto the seat behind her. We rode slowly and reached her PG.

'Take it,' she gave me a dupatta. I take it and put on my shoulder. 'What are you doing? Wrap it like Muslim girls do,' she instructs me.

'Is it okay?'

'Yeah, now act like a girl. Walk slowly. Be a girl.'

'Have you gone mad? I am not a girl how can I be a girl. Leave me on the footpath, I will be okay there.' I said.

'Okay at least you can cover your mouth, no?'

She took her handbag and faced the reception. She filed her entry and took her entrance slip. The receptionist was staring at me. She held my waist again and I got to the first floor.

'Is this it?' I asked gasping.

'No, third floor.'

'Fuck!' I pulled her aside and misbalanced. But she did what I never expected. She held me tight and smiled.

'I'm your walking stick Mr. Don't worry, put your hand on my shoulder,' she smiled.

'Take off your dark glasses, it's night,' I changed the topic. She removed the goggles and tucks a wisp of hair behind a ear. 'Let it be, it's looking nice.'

'Mr. Vicky stop flirting. I am not your girlfriend,' she smiled and covered her head with the same dupatta.

'When did I say that? Thank God you're not my girlfriend,' I couldn't afford the expensive stuff she was eating or wearing.

'I don't date the losers,' she said.

'I'm not a loser, I have everything.' *I had recently lost something most precious.*

'Have you a girlfriend?'

'Is a girlfriend the necessity to be alive?' *Yeah for me it is, of course.*

'Tell me - yes or no.'

'No. Not yet.' *She will always be mine.*

'Really?' we reached the third floor. I didn't reply. She unlocked the palace-type room. 'My roommate is not here, you can use her bed.'

'Thanks.'

She smiled and gathered the bra-panties piled on the bed. A room with pink distemper walls covered with cool dudes and hotties. A big Godrej almirah, a pink colored laptop and two separate beds with pink coverlets. *I don't know why she chose pink the most.*

I sat down on the bed and untied my shoes. 'Your socks smell? If yes, then please throw them outside.'

'No, I wear branded socks,' I said though I knew that even my clothes were filthy and cheap.

'Ho! Ho! Look at your clothes! They look unwashed! Anyway, who cares whether the socks is Jockey. No one will grab your legs to see them. People are smart here, they will understand your category by seeing you.' She did maa-bahan in single statement.

'We are a middle-class family, not like you,' I said.

'Then what is the need to show off by saying branded or Jockey? You looking cool even in a dirty pant-shirt,' she winked. I lowered my head and smiled.

'Finally,' she said.

'What?'

'Your smile,' she smiles back. 'Rest here. I'm arranging dinner for you.'

She had changed into a pink jersey with yellow stripes and left the room. The room was neat and well-done up. I checked out her laptop. Dell Vostro, the same as what I use but protected with a password. I crack it, the Windows opened and the desktop screen was visible. It was clean, just like her room. No unwanted objects like romantic songs, selfies, my computer and recycle bin icons. I opened the folder name *important files> assignment> fsbfm>sjhsdf>sdvah> and it ended up with adult films.* What if God divided us into male or female, dirty thoughts lead same way.

Divyanshi entered with two large plates filled with rice.

'You opened it! How do you know the password?' she asked.

'It was easy.'

'How?'

'You had provided a *hint* below the password - 'pink angel'. So I tried various combinations and got to 'angel pink' which worked,' I simply told her.

Girls are *zero* in knowledge of computer and they score above ninety. And boys score barely forty and can hack ISI secrets. We ate and chatted.

'So, what's the matter?' she said, licking rice from her fingers.

'What matter?' I asked, my mouth full.

'Girlfriend. You said you don't have a girlfriend.'

'But I don't have one.' I actually don't want to remember Kanchan anymore. The rice was delicious.

'Himanshu Sharma,' she spoke.

'Who?'

'My boyfriend,' she said.

'Oh!'

'Actually my ex.'

'Good,' I said. I don't know why but I did. A boy cannot see another boy with a girlfriend like Divyanshi.

'He kicked my ass.'

'I'm so sorry.'

'He did whatever he wanted; wasted my money, abused me, fucked me and finally threw me out.'

'Such an asshole.'

'All boys are the same dear. I cannot believe how they can leave someone so easily, the one who loves them most,' she wiped her mouth.

'Yeah everyone else.' I favored.

'And you?'

'I? I am good.'

'What's your story? Tell me yaar, your face says that you have lost someone,' she said.

'I too had a love story.'

'Great!'

'But we broke up the first week of this month.'

'You did?' she raised an eyebrow.

'Hmm.'

'Gosh! Terrific! You guys are really assholes.' I smiled at her manners.

'I did it because we couldn't get married. We are not of the same caste. She is a good girl. But our parents are against it,' I finished my portion and she offered me her own. I refused.

She looked surprised.

'Yeah!' I said, 'You are from Chennai and people there can have love-marriages. But in Haryana, we marry and then love.'

'People in Chennai cannot have love marriages as well,' she said gloomy.

'Really?'

'Papa is forcing me to marry his best friend's son who lives in Dubai. I cannot marry a man I have never seen in my whole life.'

'And Himanshu? Do you think he was a good man to marry?'

'He is an asshole, I already told you. I will not marry him if he comes into my life again. He even blocked me on FB. How dare he? I have eight hundred plus friends on Facebook and the maximum numbers are boys. I can find one boyfriend among them!' She was talking nonsense, but it did not matter what she said. She was hiding her emotions by this nonsense. Everybody does.

'Add me as your friend,' I said and she smiled.

'Vodka?' she offered me, unbelievably at that point.

I shook my head - there was no place in stomach for liquid. She pulled out a bottle of vodka from her wardrobe. My mouth watered.

'I know you drink yaar - be a part of my restless night. I cannot sleep at nights without liquor.'

'I'll vomit dear. My stomach is really full.'

'Mine too, but only two pegs okay?'

'Okay.'

She had much more than the average Indian girl in that almirah. Pink dresses and teddy bears were common but bhujiya, vodka, soda and classic menthol were unusual.

'I'll take it with water and you?' I said when she was pouring into the glasses. 'There is ninety two percent water in human body.' She said cheers and gulped her glass down. She made a face that could tell the taste of Vodka.

'So what's the matter?' I sipped.

'The matter can be anything if you are not the daughter of your father.'

'What does that mean?'

35

'Papa passed away when I was all of three. Mom was a receptionist in a software company in Bangalore where papa was an engineer. Mom fell in love with Mr. Iyer after papa's death. Five years later, they moved to Delhi. Mom gave a birth to baby boy. Both mom and Mr. Iyer were happy but I was left out. I love my brother but Mr. Iyer prevented me to touch him. Mom was good, she let me play with him.' Divyanshi poured another one.

'Why are you calling him Mr. Iyer - after all, he is your dad?'

'Because he never proved himself my dad. My real surname is Malhotra. When I turned to fifteen, mom also passed away in an accident. Manju, my brother, went Bangalore for his education. At the age of twenty, I fell in love with Himanshu, my neighbor, to avoid loneliness. He was a good-looking boy. He always stared me when we crossed each other. One day, he proposed to me. I really loved him. One day, Mr. Iyer saw us talking on our roof. First he beat me with a plastic pipe and then he locked me in a room. He neither opened the door nor gave me food for two days. And when he opened it, he showed me photos of the Dubai guy. I refused to marry him and left the home. When I tried to call Himanshu he didn't take my calls. I tried to contact him on FB, but he blocked me. That meant that he was not interested in me anymore. Two days inside the room and my only hope was Himanshu. I was really mad for him. Now I'm here with only mom's savings that are invested,' she said weeping.

'Kanchan's mom also beat her with plastic pipes,' I said.

'Who?' Divyanshi surprisingly asks.

'Oh! I'm sorry. I forgot to tell you about Kanchan. She was my girlfriend,' I said. 'Was?' she said. 'I broke up with her one month ago.'

'Why?' She gulped one more peg.

'Because she was a good girl. And she knew how to love.'

'Yeah! Of course, she was. But what is the reason you are not together?' She takes a handful of bhujiya.

'We cannot get married, I told you already.'

'Yes I know, but why? I don't think caste differences and religion stop you from loving anyone.'

'They not stop you from loving anyone. But you marry whoever whenever your parents want,' I take a sip. She was pouring her third one.

'You know Vicky, you are so sweet. You sacrifice your love for your family. And I left my family for love.' She sounded tired.

'Papa is not talking to me. Maa does not wanna see my face. They don't care about me any longer.' I said emotionally.

'Even you have parents.'

I nodded.

'Go home and say sorry,' she held my hands.

'I cannot yaar. Papa says that if you come home I'll cut you into pieces.'

'He is joking. No parents will kill their children.'

Joke is when if a dead body shakes leg. She was unaware about *honour killings.* Haryana, it is well-known for it. Everyday a new story comes to light; someone killed their daughter, another, their only son, a boy found hanging on a fan, a father killed his daughter and her boyfriend... I could see my future.

'Hello,' Divyanshi snaps her fingers. 'Marry her.'

'Have you gone mad?'

'Stupid! If your family has already rejected you, why are you spoiling Kanchan's life? Go and marry her fool. 'Her eyes were dull as she said this but mine became bright. She was right.

'Really!'

'Yeah, rascal just go. Not everyone is lucky like you. I know how it feels when you lose someone special.'

A tear rolled down her eyes and I wiped it. The next moment she hugged me tight. Her emotions were flying in tears. That is what I want to see in every girl. Emotions are part of a human being and if you show them then you are a human.

Divyanshi was still on my lap. I grabbed her face and wiped her tears again. Her eyes turned wet and a wisp of hair covered her left eye. I placed it behind the ear. We make then eye contact and I could see love in those big eyes. I was doing wrong thinking of this I removed my eyes. Then she held my face and put her lips on mine. She closed her eyes and leaned.

I was stunned but I could not get free. She moved.

'Sorry,' she said.

'It's okay,' I said after a pause. 'Actually it was good.'

A smile appeared on her face. She put her fist on my chest.

'Promise me Vicky,' she looks in my eyes.

'What?'

'You will marry with Kanchan.' She got her fingers in my finger gap again.

'And if I don't?'

'You won't. Believe me, you will get her. God cannot be that heartless. Vicky you had been lost the love of family but don't lose her,' she tightened her grip.

'Okay, I will,' I squeeze her hands softly. 'But promise me that you too, you will go home to meet your dad and Himanshu.'

'There is nothing left for me.'

'God cannot be so cruel, remember what you said.'

She smiled and again hugged me. I thought she would kiss me again. I applied saliva on lips to make them soft. But she didn't and moved towards her bed.

'Good night and sleep tight,' she said.

Sleep tight with whom? I was staring her curvy waist. It was awesome.

'Divyanshi Malhotra,' I wanted to chat with her.

'Hmm Mr. Vikram Bhatti,' she said without turning.

'Don't you think we have similarities?' I said stupidly. Actually, I wanted to hear her voice - it reminded me of Kanchan.

'Similarities like what?' She finally turned and now we were facing each other. Her long and straight nose was almost touching my thick and tiny one.

'We have nothing in common,' I said and she laughed. Vodka reached in my nostrils.

'We have everything but love,' she put her right hand on me.

'But I have nothing. No family, no friends, no girlfriend and no money,' I placed my hand on her waist.

'We are friends, no? And money is not that much of a need.'

'You have it so you can say that. I know how I passed these thirty days.'

'Complete your graduation, find a job and marry her. Face difficulties - don't run from them,' she said.

'It's not that simple. Without money I cannot support myself for long.'

'You need a stick to stand, not money.'

'Why don't you marry me,' I chuckled.

'I had already said that I don't date losers.'

'But you can kiss a loser!' I laughed. She smiled in reply. She threw a blanket over me and then covered herself with another. She was caring and loving like Kanchan, but more beautiful. 'Good night Divya,' I said and turned.

'Good night sweet dreams.' I hate who show their back.

Early next morning, before sunup, she left me for ISBT and I moved back to Ambala.

36

'Hello!'

'Who are you and why are you calling me?'

'This is Vicky.'

'Vicky who?'

'Sweety please give the phone to Kanchan.' Kanchan's mobile was switched off. When I dialed Sweety she behaved like a bitch.

'There is no Kanchan and please don't call me,' she hung up.

I was trying Kanchan for the last two days after the Delhi incident. Divyanshi had been calling me to learn of Kanchan's reply.

I called again, 'Sweety, please I begging you.'

'Vicky,' and I heard the voice of my angel. She spoke my name three or four times. My words halted in my throat. I was hearing her sweet voice. It was really amazing.

'Kanchan,' I said slowly.

'Hi Vicky.'

'How's you doll?'

'I'm good now. What about you?' she said.

'Missed you.'

'Thanks.'

'And you?'

'I didn't miss you,' she said.

'Oh!'

'I've your photo. I look at it whenever I miss you.'

'I love you Kanchan.'

'I love you too,' she said and a smile came on my face. I wanted cuddles right now.

'I wanna meet you. Where are you? Come as fast as you can. I am dying to see you.'

'I'm coming Vicky,' she hung up.

I wiped my eyes and jumped over to Hritik and Sid. They were smiling. I dressed up and hid my plastered leg. Pain has been blurred in joy.

Fifteen minutes later, I heard the jingle of her anklets. My heartbeat raced. I looked up to see her. With jingling ghoonghroos she was slowly stepping ahead. I turned up to her clothes and then neck, chin, dry lips and eyes… and was stunned!

Her eyes were red with black circles below. I was staring at her with open mouth. Heart was pumping fast. She looked shabby. She was beautiful no more. The nose ring had been replaced with a silver pin. Black gaani was missing from her neck. Beautiful almond eyes were not looking attractive. She had changed.

She came close and sat on a chair next to me. I was still looking into her eyes.

'Hi Vicky,' she said slowly.

'What have you done with yourself?' My words were sad.

'I did? You did it Vicky,' she said.

'Kanchan, I'm sorry,' a tear rolled down.

'It's okay,' she said. By now, I was sobbing. She held me with both hands as I sobbed on her chest.

'I'm sorry Kanchan, please forgive me.' The tears were unstoppable. I was unable to control them.

'Shh! Quiet! I was never angry with you. You did whatever your heart said,' she wiped her tears and then mine.

'I love you baby,' I said.

'Love you too sweety.' She again put my head on her chest. I grabbed her slim waist.

'I'll never repeat it again.'

'Yeah I know.'

'I'll keep you in my pocket.'

'How sweet,' a smile came on her wan face.

'Thanks for coming darling and now please switch on your mobile,' I said.

'I came here, because I had to come.'

'Thanks love,' I smiled.

'Please Vicky forgive me for whatever I did.'

'It's okay doll. You were right, I cannot live without you.'

'No Vicky, forgive me for what I have done after you left.' Her eyes were getting wet.

'What?' my heartbeats almost stopped.

'This is for you,' she gave me an envelope. I opened it - I was not in the mood to handle a surprise gift. A ring was inside and so was a card. It was the one I had gifted her - the ten rupee one. I pulled the card out - it said, Kanchan weds … I couldn't read it anymore. I was frozen. I needed water. She moved towards the gate.

The phone rang - it was Divyanshi, 'Give me good news.'

'She is getting married.'

'Wow! Congrats.'

'Not to me.'

'What? Didn't you ask her to elope?' she asked angrily.

'She handed me her marriage invitation card,' I said.

'Give me her number. I'll talk to her.'

'This is Haryana - if you talk to a girl about her BF she will take it badly,' I said.

'I'll say that I'm your friend,' she said.

'A girl and boy can never be friends, in her opinion.' I was getting tired.

'Then I'll become your sister,' she was treating it as a joke. Here, I was dying inside.

'That's why I'm asking you not to talk to her.'

'Then ask her to run away with you and have a court marriage,' she said.

'I'll talk to you later,' I hung up.

37

'We will be your witnesses and you can persuade even your class girls, no. Sangeeta, Harry and Khushi,' Sid said.

'We can just call Divyanshi,' Hritik said.

'Let it be yaar. She is getting married and I don't think she will be ready to elope,' I said.

My buddies were consoling me and giving me ideas. They thought that it is simple elope with a girl from a conservative family. Even if she consented, how would I take her to Chandigarh?

Second, after our marriage how would we eat? I was not a son of a billionaire. But my friends were irrepressible.

'She will be ready if you have the guts to ask her,' Hritik shouted.

'I've guts dude but what about family respect?' I said.

'What family, which family? You don't have any family other than us,' Hritik said placing his hand on my shoulder.

'It's all happening only because of you.' Yeah! He was. Neither had he called my papa nor did he throw me out of his life.

'It's because I couldn't see you commit suicide. You are a more than a brother.' He hugged me.

'Oye! Stop this brotherhood cuddling-wuddling. Tell me clear, you elope or not?' Gujjar showed Gujjargiri.

The list of sins was increasing day-by-day since my patch-up with Kanchan. I fell in love was my first sin. It was a sin obviously because she deserved not Vicky. Second, to love her like freak. And third one I was preparing recently. Elope with an innocent girl. After a long pause I said, 'yes.'

Now this was the time for preparation and planning. Sid gathers sack and placed them aside. Hritik threw pen and diary in my lap.

'Write down the points,' he shut the door.

'Okay,' I confusingly nodded.

'First, you will convince Kanchan to run. Fix a date, say next Monday. Early, at three or four in the morning, I'll arrange taxi and wait at the bus stand. You'll come with her at the exact time. We'll be in Chandigarh high court soon,' that was Hritik's master plan. 'Oh sorry, I forgot I tell you the most important thing, buy sleeping pills for her. Strictly instruct her to dissolve them in dinner. And she will not eat that food.

'I think it's perfect,' Sid Gujjar gave a thumbs up.

I nodded.

Now how was I to convince Kanchan? It was the biggest issue.

'The government has a policy.' Hritik took out a diary.

'About what?' I asked.

'If you marry a lower caste girl you get security in the form of two constables for one year and ninety thousand rupees to invest,' he said.

'Really?' Sid's eyes widened.

'Yeah I read it too somewhere.' I said.

'It means that if you do not have a job, you can marry one girl for one year and then leave; marry another girl and so on. Wow!' he added and now our eyes widened.

'No,' I said.

'Hritik is this applicable if you elope with your brother's saali,' Sid asked.

'Stop yaar,' I closed my eyes and stuck my head on my pillow.

'Even our government supports lovers then why not parents?' Hritik paused. I could understand his pain. Ritika was also getting married in the next two months.

'You know, Anjani's brother wants me to marry his sister. But papa....,' Sid closed his eyes.

'Why don't you both try to talk with your respective parents? Convince them,' I said.

'Being from the same village is my problem,' Hritik said. He was right - we cannot wed a girl even if she is from the next village to ours. Marriage with a girl from the same village was impossible.

'And my dad, he is Hitler. I cannot disobey him ever,' Sid said.

Only convince Kanchan was not the proper solution, I thought deeply.

My phone rang.

'Hi,' I said.

'Hey sweety, how's you?' It was Divyanshi.

'I'm good now.'

'Good. So?'

'So what?' I murmured.

'What's next?'

'Elope.'

'Wow! Ummmaaahhh…? She gave me a long phone kiss.

'Thanks.'

'Don't forget my testimony. I want to see you before you go to hell,' she laughed aloud.

'Of course.' I smiled and hung up.

38

'Will you elope or not?'

'Try to understand Vicky, I cannot.'

'Okay then.'

'Vicky! Why you behaving like shit. You are fully responsible for this situation,' Kanchan caught my hands.

We were in the backyard of her home. Aunty had an appointment, Sweety was in school and Amma was in her room. Kanchan called me to meet me one last time before her marriage. She was looking good. May be she wanted to talk more about us but as always I thought about myself only.

'Please baby. I know I was wrong, I did everything wrong with you. But my intention was to make you feel happy. Are you happy?'

'No,' she said.

'Then how can I be happy? I never spend a single day without thinking of you. Now please let's elope.'

'What about my family?'

'I lost mine for you,' I said .She said nothing.

Her marriage was only thirteen days away and I convinced her. I kissed her dry lips and left. She was happy. I never thought of her family at all.

I had never tried to convince my family. I was afraid that they would reject me. If I showed some guts then perhaps my family would let me go back? But then, I gave up Kanchan and they rejected me as well.

Now I have half a Kanchan and no parents.

I make a call to Kanchan.

'Hmm,' she spoke.

'Baby listen to me carefully - I'm going home today and when I'll return, we will make plans to elope. We will do it two days before your marriage. Take care bye.'

I left for Ambala to meet Jai. Jai, best friend of Jeet who could even die for him.

'Hello bro,' I raised a hand.

'Hello,' we shook hands..

'Bro I've a request and hope you will agree,' I caught his hand with my second one.

'Tell me.'

'I need Preety's contact number. Please don't say no, I know that you are still talking to your girlfriend.' Jai's girlfriend was best friend of Jeet's girlfriend. So, it was not an issue for Jai's girlfriend.

He was silent and then he said, 'Okay.'

I dialed but got no reply. I reached the railway station and left for home. Then she gave me a brief missed call.

'Hello Preety!' I dialed her back.

'Yes, who's this?'

'Hi, I'm Vikram, a friend. Actually I need to talk to you – tell me when you are free and alone.'

'Vikram who? I'm free.'

'Okay then. I am Jeet's friend. Why are you not talking to him?' I said.

'Listen Mr. this is our own matter. You not have to involve in it.'

'Yeah but because of you he was going to commit suicide. Means who the hell you think you are?' People were staring me.

'What?' I lied and she melted. Sometimes a lie can fix life. 'I don't have his contact no. please say him to call me right now.'

'Of course young lady.'

I straight dialed for Jeet, 'Hello *Bhosdi kay* dial a number I tell you. And don't forget to tell you are in hospital.' I told him number and hang up.

39

'Vicky!' Jolly said surprised.

'Hi!' I said.

'Maa, Vicky.' He called out to mom.

Mom came running and hugged me. Her hands were smeared in flour and now my back was smeared with it. Heavy bags became lighter. There was excitement in the household. I touched grandma's feet. My eyes were searching papa.

'Is she very beautiful?' Grandma asked. I smiled.

'Have you come here for our agreement to your marriage? If so, then there is no place for you in this house,' was mom's clear statement.

'Then why these tears?' I asked.

'Because I love you,' she said.

'And for your love you are taking all my happiness,' I said.

'This is not our culture. Happiness is, respect your elders and do what they ask you to do.'

'I did whatever you want but this is a question of my life.'

'Then go. There is nothing for you,' Mom said and her eyes again turned wet. I turned to go but Jolly stopped me. I walked past him and left home forever.

I spent the night at Charkhi Dadri railway station. I travelled to Rewari next. Ritika was waiting for me there. Yea! Ritika. I called her to fix the matter between her and Hritik.

'Vikram, are you Vikram?' A beautiful girl stood behind me.

'Ritika!' *she has a big ass.*

'Wow! You're beautiful.'

'Thanks.' She didn't know that I was getting mad for her. This is the thing I wanted to correct in my character. Each and every beautiful girl seems as my girlfriend. She was property of my best friend and my intentions were to fuck her.

'So, why did you call me here?' she asked adjusting her dupatta. *Okay, beautiful lady now I can talk to you easily.*

'I actually wanted to tell you that Hritik still loves you. He will elope if you agree.' I lied again.

'Is he ready for it?'

'Ready? Of course. He is mad for you to see you as a wife,' I lied again.

'Mom is heart patient,' she said softly.

'Listen Ritika! You cannot suffer like this forever. Parents are right but we do also have feelings. Don't you want to see Hritik as your husband or can you just marry anyone else?'

'Okay, I want some time to think over it.' she said.

'Take your time but reply before your marriage,' I said and she smiled.

'Okay' she shook my hand and moved. I was a chutiya because I didn't ask for a tea after all.

I travelled to Rohtak. I had to solve things between Veer and Shruthi. Parents of suffering lovers would hate me.

I reached Rohtak at 12:35pm. Veer was in college. I went to his house and met his mom. 'Aunty namastay,' I touched her feet.

'Namastay beta!' she did not recognize me.

'Veer's friend, Vikram.'

'Sit beta. Neeraj, make tea for brother,' she says to Veer's sister.

'Aunty, it's okay. Actually I want to tell you something. It's about Veer and Shruthi.'

Aunty looks sick.

'They have eloped?' Aunty asked.

'No.'

'Then okay, Neeraj make tea now.'

'Maa. Can I call you maa?' I asked.

'Of course beta, you are like Veer for me.' *Yeah aunty it is only until you don't know my intentions.*

'Aunty Shruthi is good girl for Veer.'

'She is more than a good girl but only if her parents come first to see Veer.'

'Aunty is it more important than a good bride? You know her family very well. Be a true mom and make your son happy. In the fight for a first come, first get you will miss a nice bahu. Boys are now committing suicide for wives these days.' My statement shakes her fully and the last line is most effective.

'I'll talk to your uncle beta,' she said.

'Thanks aunty,' I caught her hands and she smiled.

After tea I left for Kaithal, the birthplace of Sid Gujjar. His father was Gyanchand Gujjar the most respected person in the village. He was a retired Patwari. He thinks, the prime is only for enjoyment. But enjoyment should not be in your own village because it hurts the respect.

I greeted aunty and uncle while Sid's elder brother was busy with the cattle. Aunty went into the kitchen and uncle was struggling with the cot. 'Uncle may I help you!' I said.

'No, I am okay. So, how's study going on?' Uncle doesn't make eye contact.

'It's good uncle,' I replied.

'You are doing good I know, but I'm asking about my idiot one,' he said, tightening the rope.

'He is doing well too,' *doing well with American Pie series and Spider Solitaire.* I didn't say, 'Uncle what about marriage?' I said.

'Whose marriage?' Uncle faced me and I was frightened.

'Sssssid.'

'What will he do after he gets married? No one will give him a job and if he has no job, then he gets no wife in our community.'

'Community!' I whispered. 'No Uncle, he must get a job.'

'Okay, now come to the point.' He understood there was more to come.

'Anjani is a good girl, no?' I said.

'No. Anyway how do you know Anjani? Did Sid tell you about her?'

'No.... actually... I...'

'Yeah speak up,' uncle was getting heavy on me.

'Vikram, come take tea with me,' aunty's voice brings some relief.

'I am coming aunty,' I got up and hurried inside.It was hard to spend time with uncle. *Thanks aunty.* Sid's brother and I were in farms. The breeze was cheering up the body. I thought about Kanchan, she was not calling me after our last conversation. I tried her number but it was switched off.

Sid's brother and I finished dinner while uncle was in his bedroom watching news. I went slowly and sat near him.

'Vikram!' he said.

'Yeah uncle,' I smiled.

'Dinner done?'

'Hmm yes,' I said.

Uncle remained silent and focusing on the news. But I don't think he was really watching it. Then he said, 'You know Vikram, that family has many problems. A parents-less daughter cannot become a good bahu. My elder bahu divorced my elder son and settled down with a drunk. They deserve only that type of people who hurt them.' Uncle shared his pain. And in his pain there was love and caring for his son.

'You are right uncle but Anjani called you *Papa.* Don't you think that both those sisters are not similar? She loves you as a papa because she was really missing her papa. A true bahu treats a father-in-law as a father.' I finished my part and left his room.

Early next morning I left for Ambala. Now I was feeling relaxed. Everything will be good in a short time as I wished. I was still missing Kanchan and her missed calls. I had to plane my elopement now.

40

'Bhai, thank you,' it was Jeet.

'For what?' I was in deep sleep.

'For persuading Preety for me.'

'It's okay dude but don't forget my treat,' I said rubbing my eyes. It was seven in morning.

'Sure bro,' he said and hung up.

It was the third day that I did not get a call from Kanchan. I wanted to see Kanchan badly and decided to visit her home. Only ten days left for her marriage. Her house was crowded with beautiful aunties and native girls. Thank God no one known to me was there.

'Vicky!' a voice reached my ears. I turned and see a beautiful girl right behind in a red sari. I didn't recognize her.

'Yeah! Who are you?' I said.

'Sancheeta, Kanchan's cousin. Actually I saw you in a photo in her personal bag. Come, she was waiting for you. Thank God maami ji is not here. You know, I was really missing you in her marriage. To being in girlfriend's marriage has a different joy, is it not. Sorry, I am a little loud-mouthed. She is in her room - talk to her.' Thank God she kept quite otherwise I would choke a cloth in her mouth.

'Baby,' I said and she turned. My mouth dropped open. She was looking fabulous. The dark circles had gone, the nose ring was back and black gaani on white skin added extra stars on beauty. She smiled and hugged me tight. The peacock colored suit without a duppatta was perfect. 'Why didn't you call me Kanchan?' Her head was on my shoulder.

'I did Vicky. But mom took my phone away. I missed you darling.'

'Time to go sweet lady. I came here to see you once. By the way you have many cousins. Take one of their mobiles and call me.' I whispered into her ear and kissed her white cheek.

'You kissed her? You know, when I was getting married my boyfriend fucked me on the last night. If you are preparing for it I can help you.' Sancheeta spoke again.

'Thanks, but we will convert it into honeymoon.' I said and her remained open.

'Sancheeta please,' Kanchan said.

'What? Look at him he is cute. Why don't you marry him?' Sancheeta shouts.

'Because of our castes. You know very well,' Kanchan said.

'Fuck the caste. Elope, the simplest way!' she stole my words.

'Yeah that's what I say.' I jumped in ladies.

'Vicky, you go now and I will not elope with you,' she winked.

'Then whom will you elope with, your husband?' Loud-mouthed again barked.

'Why didn't you marry with your boyfriend?' Kanchan said. War starts between the cat and the bitch.

'Because he was not rich and neither has a bike nor white shirt. He was tenth failed,' Sancheeta faced down in grief.

'Then why you loved him?' I asked shockingly.

'Because he has big monster in his pan....t.'

'Okay! Okay! Sancheeta please. He is my boyfriend and I don't want him to fuck you,' Kanchan said and I was astonished.

'Really, he can?' she wide opened her big eyes.

'Vicky please, mom can be here anytime.' Kanchan pleaded.

'Bye Vicky. Don't forget this *saali*, I can be your *aadhi-gharwali*,' lust was flickering in her eyes.

I left before that bitch could bite me.

At home, more good news was waiting for me. Veer came with a sweet box. He hugged me.

'Thanks yaar,' he said.

'Anytime buddy,' I whispered.

'Mom and dad are going next Monday with sagun. This will be the most precious gift you could give me.' He almost cried.

'Now it's not time for tears.' I smiled and his eyes glittered again.

'What about you and Kanchan?'

'We are planning...'

'Do it fast, otherwise she and her husband will plan their honeymoon. It was a joke for him, but for me it was pain.

'Let's see,' I faked a smile.

When you do not smile with your heart it appears on your face. And in a while he understood what I feel. His intention was not to make me feel bad so he apologized. But the heart has already gone in deep thinks. I need to talk right now to the people who understood me. And he or she can be anyone of my close one like Kanchan, Hritik or Divyanshi.

I called Divyanshi. We had not been in touch for some time. I don't want a tag of selfishness. Divyanshi cares for me means there must be a responsibility for me as well.

'Hey smarty, don't say that you are missing me.' Divyanshi understood me as I told.

'So much,' *I truly did.*

'How's Kanchan? I have to tell you something. But first I want to hear good news,' she said.

'She is fine. Now you tell me.'

'I met papa,' she said *papa* for first time.

'Really? What did he say?'

'He doesn't wanna see my face again. But I did a good job, you know what?'

'What?' I asked.

'I met Manju and he is cute. He called me akka for the first time. He demanded a raakhi on raksha-bandhan.' She laughed but I knew that she hid her emotions.

'Divya.'

'Hmm.'

'Cry,' I said because tears overcome pain.

'I can weep, but there is no one to wipe my tears.' After your marriage you must come to Delhi and I will cry aloud.' She smiled for sure.

41

Ritika was ready to elope with Hritik but I made a mistake that could shake trust of Hritik. I didn't tell him anything about my meeting with her. I convince Ritika to come Chandigarh the same day when Kanchan and I were getting married. She will come I knew but I was jolted what if Hritik refused?

And here the fight starts between good and evil thoughts of my mind:

"Then I will marry with her," evil said.

"Oh! And what about our Kanchan," good said.

"Don't forget one on one free, deal is good," evil laughed.

"Fuck you! You think we are able to handle both at one time? They are sex goddess, will torn us into pieces." Good advised.

"I will manage. Look at Ritika and her stuff." Evil lusts.

"Look at our Kanchan she is cute," good is caring.

"Kanchan is yours, mine are beautiful chicks." Evil trespassed.

"But Kanchan is our love." And good thoughts once again lost.

With all the evil and good conversation I received a call from Kanchan. 'Hello baby,' I said.

'It's me!' It was aunty! I kept calm. But she said again, 'Vicky have you gone mad?'

'What happened?'

'Come to my home - I have to tell you something.'

'No, say whatever you want on the phone,' I said.

'Have you any respect for me in your heart? If yes, then Vicky please let her go. I'm joining my hands in pleading for this. You know beta, I'm a heart patient and if this happens I will die. No one will marry my sons. Sweety's life will be spoilt.' Aunty began weeping.

'Aunty I love her,' I said finally.

'Yes I know beta, but I gave you a chance. Now I have arranged everything for the wedding. I know Kanchan will run away with you, she is mad. But you? You also have a sister, think about her. I don't have the courage to cancel this marriage.' I couldn't speak.

'Who told you that we are going to elope?' I asked after a long pause.

'That day when you called Kanchan. It was Sweety who took your call that day. She told me the whole matter yesterday. I beat Kanchan many times but she is mad for you. Please Vicky, if you have a heart then save my family.' Aunty said.

I found her strange. She cared for family dignity more than she did her daughter. I decided against hurting her family.

The next day came as planned but the characters had changed. Ritika was waiting for us in Chandigarh. She was in college as far as her parents knew. Everything went according to plan. Kanchan was calling me again and again but I switched off my mobile phone. Sid and Hritik were at the bus stand with a taxi.

'Where is Kanchan?' Sid asked.

'She is not coming,' I said.

'What?' Both screamed.

'Yeah! I'm gonna marry Divyanshi. Let's move.' I lied again. People believe lies easily and question truths.

Early morning we were in the Chandigarh High Court. I found Ritika. She came and hugged Hritik from behind. She thought that he was waiting for her.

'Bro, tell her that I am not Vick.....' he turned and was shocked, 'What is she doing here? I thought she was Divyanshi.'

'What?' Ritika glared me, 'And who is this Divyanshi?'

'Hold on, listen guys.' I tried to stop them.

'What listen, chutiye?' Hritik said wept almost.

'Sorry bro, I didn't tell you but you have to marry her right now,' I said.

'I won't.'

'Ritika when you come?' Sid came with the varmalas. 'You are looking hot.'

'Thanks, hey Vicky clear the matter. You were saying that he is dying without me,' Ritika said sarcastically.

'Yes, I am dying without you,' Hritik jumps into the conversation.

'Good, then marry her and save yourself,' I said.

'No am not going to marry her without my family's permission,' Hritik said.

'Wow! And you think they will come and give you *aashirwad* for a long life. Forget about it - her parents are searching for her everywhere,' I said.

'Then who will marry me?' Ritika cried.

'I do, see I have varmala also,' Sid shows her a plastic bag.

'Fuck off Sid,' Ritika said irritatingly.

After a long squabble Hritik agreed to the wedding. Then Hritik got a call from his dad.

'See your lovely girlfriend has ran away with someone. I told you she is not a good girl. Bloody characterless,' Dad said.

'Papa she is with me, we got married today,' son said.

'You cannot be my son. If I see you anywhere I will kill you both.' Dad said angrily.

'Papa we have security for one year,' son said.

'Live for one year,' said Dad and hung up.

'Vicky I will kill you,' Hritik grabbed my collar. 'I thought only you understand me but you fired my whole life ....'

'I understand you so that I did at all. Hritik one year later everything will settle down,' I said. We return and Kanchan had gone with her husband. I enjoyed the day with my buddies but the night was not so good. The room was looking haunted, food taste was fainted and heartbeat was increasing whenever I thought about her honeymoon. Eyes were getting wet.

Sid Gujjar came with a bottle of Royal Stag. He was also crying. We finished a full bottle between us. Hritik and Ritika were in his room, for their first night together as newlyweds.

42

I woke up at seven. Sid was not there. I rubbed my eyes and saw that the whole street was busy. People were going and coming from both sides. I ran downstairs. Gujjar was on cot. I went close and asked the problem.

'You have to be tough,' he said sadly.

'I'm tough enough.'

'Then toughest,' his voice stuck in his throat. 'What's the matter yaar?' I rubbed my eyes.

'Bro, you made a big mistake.'

'Yes. I know.'

'Big mistake like never before.' 'Anything else,' I moved towards wash basin. 'Kanchan.........' and he stopped.

'Kanchan what?' I turned back.

'She committed suicide,' he said as fast as earth slipped for me. I ran to the gate but he caught me. 'Don't go Vicky, her family will kill you.'

I didn't care. Ritika and Hritik had already reached her home. People were staring me angrily. Tears were rolling down, my legs were pulling me. I collapsed, stood up, ran and finally reached her home. Doom was ready to go. Beautiful lady was twisted into white and red shroud. I fell down there, knees were broken up, throat dehydrated, eyes red and ears were hearing blubbering people. Four men lifted her body and passed by me.

I was crying about my last decision. Why didn't I elope with her as planned? I scream and everybody stops to hear it. Hritik runs and helps me get up. Every lovely moment with her was in front of me. With closed eyes I was feeling her presence and laughing face.

The day I left many things; friends, college, degree, family, Kanchan and that city. I had been lost every single thing in my life. The dignity and caste system gulped another love story.

Six months after her death she is still fresh in my heart. I drink because I cannot sleep at nights. Her laughing face always makes me cry.

My friends are rum and beer. These help me forget Kanchan. Divyanshi pays for my room. She has completed her graduation and works in a BPO. Fifteenth February is Kanchan's birthday. Three days to go.

Arun also wept. He stood up and hugged me. 'I'm sorry bhai.'

'It's okay now. Cheer up!' I said and wiped his eyes.

He remained silent for the next five minutes and then asked, 'What happened to Sid Gujjar?'

'He got married to Anjani,' I said.

'How? His father was not for it, is it not?'

'Hmm, but he later agreed. He didn't wanna lose his son unlike my dad,' I said.

Arun left for Delhi with wet eyes.

Epilogue

Jeet loves his girlfriend and she loves him more than her puppy. He works in DLF Gurgaon. Hritik is a successful lecturer in the college where we studied. Ritika runs an aanganwadi. Sid and Anjani are happy and enjoying their married lives. Unfortunately he didn't get a good job but became a good farmer. Harmender is servant of Google India and earns money and fat equally.

Jolly got a charming and adorable wife and is having two sweet babies. He is working in CNC in Gurgaon too.

Sweety is a sweeper at Punjab National Bank and is flirting with an accountant of age thirty and a manager of age fifty. Aunty still visits doctors. No one knows the exact disease. Maybe she needs to change either the doctors or blood. Amandeep's curse came true and she finally is happy.

Navita Smriti, and Paramjeet are blurred faces now.

Mommy, papa now love only their grandchildren and not me. Mom calls her grandson by my name. Grandma gets pension set up by grandpa. Bhabhi even doesn't know who I am? Jolly calls once in a week or month and we talk about family.

Divyanshi is working in a call center and advises me to join her. She has sold her Scooty and has purchased a brand new bicycle. So that she can pay for rooms and dessert and it doesn't drink petrol too.

And I, I have nothing of mine. I am that I was. I have no job, no experience to run a house. The whole day I spend with novels and magazines. Divyanshi instructs me to write but I don't think I can write… and what could I write after all?

Valentine's Day she comes with flowers, sweeps the room, purchases brand new clothes for me. She threw out the empty bottles and lit agarbatti. She left the next morning and an envelope was below my pillow. It was a Valentine special and says:

Dear Vikram,

I know today is day for lovers but for me every day is attached with you. I will come to the point directly. I love you. It's Kanchan's birthday. You have to forget her. Joy and sorrow are two phases of life. If you laugh in joy once, then cry in sorrow once as well. So enjoy and Happy Valentine's Day!

Best wishes

Divya'

It was ten in the morning. Kanchan's birthday is special for me indeed. Finally I dialed Divyanshi, 'Divya…Will you marry me?'